FAR-FLUNG

Also by Peter Cameron

LEAP YEAR

ONE WAY OR ANOTHER

FAR-FLUNG

STORIES

PETER CAMERON

HarperCollins*Publishers*

FIRST EDITION

Designed by Alma Orenstein

Library of Congress Cataloging-in-Publication Data

Cameron, Peter.
    Far-flung : stories/by Peter Cameron. —1st ed.
      p. cm.
    Contents: Just relax—The near future—The middle of everything—The secret dog—The café hysteria—Not the point—What?—Slowly—The meeting and greeting area—The half you don't know—Everywhere and no place—The winter bazaar
    ISBN 0-06-016717-3
    I. Title
PS3553.A4344F3 1991
813'.54—dc20 90-56359

91 92 93 94 95 RRD 10 9 8 7 6 5 4 3 2 1

ACKNOWLEDGMENTS

Some of these stories originally appeared, sometimes with different titles, in the following magazines: "Slowly" and "The Winter Bazaar" in *The New Yorker*, "Not the Point" in *The Mississippi Review*, "Just Relax" in *Rolling Stone*, "The Middle of Everything" in *The Paris Review*, "The Near Future" in *Columbia*, "The Secret Dog" in *The Kenyon Review*, "The Café Hysteria" in *The Quarterly*, "What?" in *Vox*, "The Half You Don't Know" in *Bostonia*, and "The Meeting and Greeting Area" in *Antioch Review*.

The writing of this book was supported by the National Endowment for the Arts, the MacDowell Colony, and The Corporation of Yaddo. The author wishes to express his gratitude to those organizations and the following individuals: Victoria Kohn, Sheila McCullough, and Jim Harms.

For
ANDY

CONTENTS

This is a work of fiction, and all characters
and incidents are imaginary.

PART I

~~~~~~~~~

I now hasten to the more moving part of my story.
I shall relate events, that impressed me with feelings
which, from what I had been, have made me what I am.

—MARY SHELLEY, *FRANKENSTEIN*

JUST RELAX

It all started at the airport. My mother had promised to pick me up, but she wasn't there. Then I was informed that the airline had lost my luggage somewhere between Zaire and New York, and right after I finished filling out a three-page claim form my younger sister, Daria, and her boyfriend, Charles, appeared and told me that my mother had become a performance artist and sold her apartment, and that I could stay with them for ten days, and after that I'd have to find my own place or go to L.A. and live with my father. Then Charles and Daria had a fight about how to get home from the airport: Daria wanted to take a cab, but Charles thought we should take some special express bus. They were so angry at each other that Daria got in a cab and Charles got on the bus, and before I could get in either they were both gone. I met an Argentine businessman, and we shared a cab back to the city; halfway there he asked the cabbie to pull over, and in the parking lot of a mall in Queens he and the cabbie snorted coke the man had just smuggled into the country. It was then that I started missing the Peace Corps.

The coked-up businessman got out of the cab at the Waldorf-Astoria. He invited me up to his room, but I told him I had contracted a disease in Africa and been sent home to die. I gave the driver Daria's address and we headed downtown. He dropped me off on a very odd street. It was made of cobblestones, and it didn't have any cars parked on it, or sidewalks. None of the doors was numbered, and they weren't normal, friendly looking doors: They were steel doors with no handles or anything on them, the kind you can only open from inside. I was about to go find another taxi—I hadn't figured out where I was going to ask it to take me—when one of the doors opened and Daria and Charles walked out.

They had changed. They were obviously dressed to go out someplace fancy. Daria saw me standing in the street and said, "Oh, Lainie, great, we left a message on our machine telling you to meet us at Minnie's, but now you can just come with us. You probably never would have found it yourself, anyway."

"Who's Minnie?" I asked.

"Who's Minnie?" Charles laughed. "I know you've been in Africa, but really, Elaine. Who's Minnie?"

"Minnie's is a restaurant," Daria said. "Charles, go fetch a cab."

Charles, apparently chastened, looked down at his shoes for a moment—they were patent leather cowboy boots—and then trotted up to the corner.

Daria waited till he was out of earshot before she spoke. "I'm sorry about the airport," she said. "I know you probably think I behaved terribly, but this is a new relationship, and I think it's important to stick up for yourself right from the start, otherwise things just get so helplessly spastic. . . ."

"Do you think I could use your bathroom before we go anywhere? And shouldn't I change?"

Daria, who had been watching Charles's receding back, looked at me. "Well, you do look awful," she sighed. "We'll run up and see what we can do."

At Minnie's we found Charles sitting at a table on its own little platform, drinking a glass of champagne. Most of the tables were on their own platforms, so walking across the restaurant was a sickening experience: You kept going up a few steps, then down a few.

"Oh, champagne," squealed Daria, helping herself to a glass. "What a good idea." She kissed Charles. Charles grinned and raised his glass.

"Cheers," he said. "To a new career." He turned to me. "Welcome home, Elaine."

Even though I didn't have a glass of champagne or a new career, I thought this was awfully sweet of Charles, so I just smiled and lifted my water glass.

"Charles, you jerk, give her some champagne!" Daria said. She hit his still upraised arm, spilling some of the peach-colored liquid.

"Oh, sorry," Charles said. He reached into the bucket, extracted the dripping bottle, and poured me a glass.

"Don't you want to know what my new career is?" Daria asked.

"Oh," I said. "I thought . . ."

"No, no, guess," Daria said. "I bet she can't guess," she said to Charles.

After she was graduated from college, Daria had gotten a job as an assistant buyer at Bloomingdale's. The last I had heard, she was manager of Men's Notions: umbrellas, wallets, and sunglasses.

"Are you still at Bloomingdale's?" I asked.

"God, no," said Daria. "Really."

"Look at her face," said Charles. "It shows on her face."

I looked at Daria's face. She was flushed, and I noticed her eyebrows were unnaturally bushy and dark. Had they been dyed?

"Are you an actress?"

"Close," said Daria. "A model. I've already done two shows. One was a designer showcase."

"She wore underwear," said Charles.

"It wasn't underwear," said Daria. "It just kind of looked like underwear."

"Are you tall enough to be a model?" I asked.

"Well, not really. But it's mostly in how you carry yourself, how you move. I move very well. They're very excited about the way I move."

"Have you told Mom?"

"It was her idea. This guy who is acting as her manager also books models, and she showed him a picture of me, and we all had dinner, and he got me the shows. The first one was a little skeevy—they still haven't paid me—but the second show was completely legit. I got five hundred dollars, and they had a big buffet. Caviar. Everything."

In the ladies' room, Daria filled me in on Charles. She had met him at Bloomingdale's, when he special-ordered a sharkskin wallet. He was only nineteen, but he was very rich, and he wanted to be an actor.

Daria was applying black lipstick with a little paintbrush, peering into the mirror. I was standing next to the sink, my back against the cool tile wall. The floor and ceiling were made of mirrors, so I felt like I was floating. I was starting to feel jet-lagged, and trying to remember the last time I slept.

"Do you like Charles?" Daria asked. She looked at me in the mirror.

"I'm not sure," I said. "He seems pleasant."

"Pleasant?" Daria said. "Pleasant? Well, that's a new concept."

"Can we go home soon?" I asked. "I'm a little exhausted."

"Oh, take one of these," Daria said. She opened her bag and took out an aqua pill. "They gave us these before the show. They animate you. They aren't harmful."

"How do you know?" I asked.

"How do I know?" Daria gave me a despairing look. "Elaine, just look at me," she said. "Do I look harmed?"

We were dancing at some club. Or rather: Daria and Charles and a boy with aluminum foil gym shorts and no shirt were dancing together, and I was sitting on a chair that was shaped like a hand, sitting in the palm and leaning back against the fingers. The pill Daria had given me was having an odd effect. I kept forgetting I was myself, drifting off somewhere, only to suddenly find I was back in the hand chair. This was not completely unpleasant.

Charles and Daria trotted off the dance floor, leaving the blond boy dancing alone. He didn't seem to notice.

"Is that your beer?" Daria asked. She pointed to a Rolling Rock on the table—a little, upturned hand—next to my chair. It was half full.

"No," I said.

Daria picked it up, looked at it, then drank from it. She handed it to Charles.

"This is disgusting," he said. Nevertheless, he took a slug and offered it to me. I declined.

"Charles wants to go to Mars," Daria said. "But I want to go to Des Moines. You decide."

"Can't we just go home?" I asked.

"Home?" asked Charles, as if this were the name of some new club he hadn't yet heard of.

"But Lainie, this is your first night in New York. We wanted to make it special."

"It's been very special," I said. "I'd just like to go home."

"I suppose we could go home," said Charles, turning the idea over in his mind.

Daria took the beer bottle from him and finished it. "All right," she said. "If it's what you really want. We'll go home. But we'll stop on the way for breakfast: French Toast! Eggs Benni!"

The next morning, while Charles and Daria went to an acting class for models, I began my job search. I went out to get a newspaper, but I got stuck in the elevator. I couldn't get it to move. After about twenty minutes it started to ascend on its own accord. It stopped, and the door opened. A woman stood there with a little piggy-looking dog on a leash.

"Are you going down?" she asked.

"I'm trying to," I said. "I don't know how to work this."

The woman gave me an unfriendly look and got in the elevator. She cranked some strange handle and the elevator started to descend none too smoothly. The dog stood on the floor, snorting, and looking up at me.

"What kind of dog is that?"

"What?" the woman said.

I repeated my question.

"This dog?" the woman said, pointing to the dog, as if there were several in the elevator.

"Yes," I said.

"A bull terrier."

The elevator landed with a thud and the woman opened the gates. We were about a foot below the main floor. I stepped up and out, and so did the woman, but the dog stayed in the elevator.

"Spanky, I'm not going to pick you up," the woman said. She pulled on the leash and dragged Spanky out of the elevator. This experience didn't seem to help his breathing problem.

"Is there a paper store around here?" I asked the woman.

"A paper store?"

"To buy a newspaper? I'm looking for a job."

"Well, the last place I'd look is in a newspaper. Don't you have any connections?"

"Not really," I said. "I just got out of the Peace Corps."

"What's that?" the woman asked.

"You've never heard of the Peace Corps?"

"Is it a band?"

"No," I said. "It's this program whereby Americans are sent to help people in developing nations."

"Help them with what?"

"Different things. I helped people in Africa on a cooperative farm."

Spanky started to eat a Coke can that was lying in the gutter.

"You don't want a dog, do you?" the woman asked. "This was my ex-boyfriend's dog. The meanest thing he ever did to me was leave Spanky. Actually, it was probably the meanest thing he ever did to Spanky, too."

I felt kind of sorry for Spanky, despite his general awfulness, but I didn't feel in a position to take him. Plus, I felt as if we were digressing. "Is there a place to get a paper?" I asked.

"A paper," the woman said. "Well, I usually just grab one from outside of someone's door. But I suppose you could buy one at Igor's. For about ten million dollars, probably."

"Where's Igor's?"

"It's on the corner. The purple awning. Would you buy me some cigarettes while you're there? Igor won't let me come in anymore. Spanky messed on his floor."

"What kind?"

"Number two," the woman said.

"No, I mean what kind of cigarettes?"

"Oh, that. Gauloises."

It was when I got back in Daria's apartment with a copy of *Backstage*—the only paper Igor's carried—that I started to panic. The paper was full of ads, but they all seemed to be people advertising themselves; the only real jobs were word-processing jobs for actors "between engagements." I could type about three words a minute. On the second-to-last page was an ad that said: "NO ACTORS . . . JUST PEOPLE. No Equity, No Experience Necessary. We just want YOU. Pilgrim Acres, Massachusetts' newest theme park, needs all types for recreational acting/being. Excellent pay, benefits, more. Call now."

I called the number. "Hello," a man said.

"Is this Pilgrim Acres?" I asked.

"Yes."

"I'm calling about the ad in *Backstage*. For people?"

"Yes."

"Do you have jobs?"

"What's your dress size?"

I told him.

"Are you reasonably attractive?"

I said yes.

"Then we have a job," he said. "If you get here by five o'clock."

"Five o'clock when?"

"Tonight," he said.

When I hung up I was elated, and only a little scared. I had never been to Boston, but my mother, who grew up there, had always said it was a "small, manageable" city, and I was sure there couldn't be as many creepy people there as there seemed to be in New York. And I was proud of myself for having gotten a job in what must have been record time. I packed some of Daria's clothes—winter clothes so she couldn't accuse me of taking things she needed—and wrote her a note and went to Penn Station and took a train to Boston. I arrived at Pilgrim Acres at a quarter to five.

The next day I started work. Mr. Antonini, the man who ran the park, said Elaine wasn't a good Pilgrim name and gave me a list of suitable names to choose from. I selected Ann, but he said they already had six Anns, so I picked Clara. First I was assigned to the Apothecary's, but then two women fainted in the Bakery, and since I had been in Africa, Mr. Antonini thought maybe I'd do better in the heat and switched me.

A few nights later I was sitting on the back steps of a row house in Medford spraying a hose at a baby standing up in an inflated swimming pool. The baby's name was Dido, and I was living with his mother and father, Louisa and Curly. Curly taught American history and lifestyles at Medford High School, and Louisa was going to a school to learn how to install cable TV in people's houses. I had met Curly—he was named after the cowboy in *Oklahoma!*—at Pilgrim Acres. A lot of teachers worked there in the summer. Curly suggested I rent their attic instead of staying in the barracks-like dorms at the park. The only problem was that I didn't think Louisa liked me very much. Either that or she couldn't speak English—she spoke only Spanish to both Curly and Dido.

Dido was shrieking from pleasure (I think) as I ran the hose up and down his pink little body. Louisa was at school and Curly was in the kitchen, fixing dinner.

After a few minutes Dido's pink little body started turning blue, so I took him out of the pool, wrapped him in a towel, and took him into the kitchen. I put a fresh diaper on him, then sat him in his high chair.

The phone rang. Curly picked it up. "Hello," he said, and then, "No. We have no Lainie here. No Elaine, either. You have the wrong number."

"Wait," I said. "I think that's for me." I took the receiver out of Curly's hand. He shrugged.

"Hello," I said.

"What was that all about?" asked Daria.

"Daria," I said. I had left a message on her machine telling her where I could be reached, but I hadn't expected to hear from her so soon.

"Who answered the phone?" she asked.

"That was Curly," I said.

"Doesn't he know your name?"

"I changed my name," I said. "I'm Clara now."

"Why did you change your name?"

"It's a long story," I said.

"Well, then, some other day," said Daria. "Listen, Elaine, are you all right? I'm worried about you, just taking off like that."

"I'm fine," I said.

"Are you sure? I mean, I'm sorry if I seemed inhospitable before. If you want to come back to the city, you can stay here. It's no big deal. Why don't you come back?"

"I don't think so," I said. "I like it here."

"Well, Edith called." Edith is our mother. "She wanted to know what was happening with you, and I told her about this Pilgrim thing and I think she's coming to see you. She's performing at some hospital or something. So be warned."

"Oh, no," I said. "I don't think I'm ready for her yet."

"Are you really O.K.?" Daria asked. "Who's this Curly person?"

"He's my landlord," I said. "He works at the Pilgrim Acres."

"Oh, speaking of jobs, make sure you buy next month's *Glamour*. I'm in it."

"Congratulations," I said. "That's great."

"Yeah, well it could have been better. I'm a DON'T picture."

It was warm in the Bakery, especially in the long Pilgrim dresses we had to wear, but I liked the job. I started to forget all about the Peace Corps and indigenous fertilizers and New York and Daria, and the simple routine of bread baking—mixing the dough, letting it rise, punching it down, shaping it, setting the moist unbaked loaves out on the paddle, pushing them into the oven, removing them an hour later, and then selling warm slices to the tourists for a quarter—seemed like the best job in the world. Some mornings I'd take an early bus out and just walk around the deserted village, up and down the wooden sidewalks, past the herb garden and chicken yards, across the dirt road and around the Village Green, past the Butcher's and the Seamstress's and the Blacksmith's and the Apothecary's, then into the Bakery, where I'd start sifting and measuring the flour. Then I started staying later at night: The Bakery closed at 4:30, but I'd walk around in my Pilgrim costume, smiling at the tourists, sitting on the benches, letting them take pictures of me holding their fat fragrant babies, waiting for dark and the fireworks display they had every night. And I'd ride the late bus home, still dressed like a Pilgrim, and walk to Curly and Louisa's house, and inside they'd be lying on the couch, watching Spanish TV, and I'd walk upstairs past Dido's room, where he slept in his crib, softly illuminated by the Virgin Mary night-light, up another flight past Curly and Louisa's room, up, up into the dark, hot attic.

One day when I came back from my morning break, Becky, the Pilgrim who ran the Bakery, told me a woman had come in and asked for me. I knew it must be my mother. About noon she reappeared with a man. They both were wearing jumpsuits and sunglasses.

"Darling," my mother said. "This is Henry, my manager."

Henry nodded. He ate one of the twenty-five-cent slices.

"Can you come out for some lunch with us?" my mother asked. "I can't talk in this place."

"I've got to wait a few minutes. I have some bread in the oven."

"I'll take the bread out," said Becky. "You can go."

"Thanks," I said. I took my apron off and walked outside with my mother and Henry.

"Can't you take that costume off?" my mother asked.

"I change at home," I said.

"Where's home?"

"I'm staying with some people in Medford. Should we go to the pub?" I asked. "It's really the only place to eat here."

"Can't we go to a normal restaurant? Henry has a car."

"I'm not supposed to leave the Village," I said. "Plus I only have half an hour."

Henry said he wanted to take a look at the working windmill, and headed down Main Street. My mother and I went into the pub. From outside it looked like an old English pub—thatched roof, gables, and leaded glass windows—but inside it was set up like a cafeteria. We both got a chef's salad and sat at a plank table.

"I'm performing tonight at the Mansard House, a private clinic for alcoholic women," my mother said. "I'd ask you to come, but

I don't think I'm ready to perform in front of family yet. I've drawn on quite a lot of my unhappy experience with your father, and it might be painful for you."

"What do you do?" I asked. I couldn't picture my mother as a performance artist. After she left my father, she decided to become an actress, and I saw her once play Mrs. Cratchit in an off-Broadway musical based on *A Christmas Carol*. She sang a song called "Another Sad Christmas, Another Sad Goose."

"I really can't talk about it," my mother said. "A performance can't be explained, it has to be experienced."

"Oh," I said.

She looked at me. "Darling, I hate to see you like this. All dressed up like a Pilgrim with no place to go." She laughed, then continued. "No, really. I'm sorry. But we've got to get you out of here."

"What do you mean?" I said. "I like this job."

"Elaine, let's be serious. You can't be a Pilgrim for the rest of your life. Now, the reason I brought Henry along was so he could see you. He's been very good about helping Daria with her new career, and I'm sure he could do the same for you. I do wish you weren't wearing that dress. And the wimple! Can you take that off, so he can at least see your hair?"

"No," I said. "It's a costume. I've got to wear it as long as I'm on the grounds."

"What if we went out to the car? Does the parking lot count?"

I suddenly realized how annoying my mother was, so I said, "What's the story with Henry?"

"What do you mean?"

"Are you sleeping with him?"

"Elaine!" my mother said. "What kind of question is that?"

"Who is he? Where did you find him? He looks like a creep."

"I beg your pardon," my mother said. "But Henry is not a creep. Henry has helped turn my life around. I'd still be sitting in that roach-infested apartment if Henry hadn't taken an interest in me."

"That's another thing," I said. "Thanks for selling the apartment. What happened to all my stuff? Did you just toss it down the incinerator?"

My mother laid down her wooden fork and looked at me for a second. "You know, Elaine," she finally said, "just because you're having a little trouble shifting your life into first gear doesn't mean you have to take your frustration out on me. I am no longer the emotional quicker-picker-upper I once was. I am an adult woman pursuing her own life. I had a perfect right to do everything I've done, and if you don't approve, that's too bad. And I didn't toss your 'stuff' in the incinerator. I am paying for it to be stored in a climate controlled, mildew-free warehouse in Long Island City. So spare me."

I didn't know what to say. I wanted to get up and walk out, but something about the Pilgrim costume prohibited a dramatic exit. So I just sat there, and picked at the American cheese slices in my salad.

My mother sighed. "I'm sorry," she said. "I guess I'm a little on edge. I still get anxious about performing."

I still didn't say anything. I felt a little like I felt after I took the aqua pill Daria gave me: I had to concentrate hard to remember that I was myself, sitting there.

"Are you O.K.?" my mother asked. "Are you sure you aren't ill? Maybe you caught something in Africa. They have some terrible diseases over there, you know. Megan Foster was telling me about her sister who got bit by some fish and started to grow scales. Perhaps you should see a doctor? Are you taking vitamins?"

"I'm fine," I said. "I have to get back to work. It was nice to see you. Good luck with your performance."

"Oh, darling," my mother said. "Don't sulk. I said I was sorry. Is this some kind of Moonie thing? Have you been brainwashed?"

This time I didn't answer. I just stood up and walked out.

When I got to the Bakery I felt sick. I sat down in the back room, but the heat from the ovens made me feel worse, so I went out and sat on the shaded back stoop. Becky looked out the Dutch door. "What happened? Are you all right?" she asked.

"I feel funny," I said.

"You look terrible."

I stood up, but I felt dizzy, so I sat down again.

"Why don't you go home?" Becky said. "Take the afternoon off. Just relax."

When I arrived at Curly's and Louisa's, my key wouldn't fit in the lock. Someone had changed it. I knocked on the door. I knew someone was home because I could hear the radio playing. I kept knocking, and after a while, I used my foot too.

Louisa opened the door, but only wide enough so she could see me. She had the chain fastened. "Go away," she said. So she did speak English.

"What's the matter?" I asked. "Why did you change the lock?"

"I know about you and Curly," Louisa said. "You must go away now, before I kill you."

"What are you talking about? Where's Curly?"

"I now understand that you try to steal Curly. That you come into our happy home and try to steal him. But no way. I always suspect you." Louisa closed the door. I knocked again, but she didn't answer it. She turned the radio up.

There was a paper bag on the porch containing Daria's winter clothes. I left them there. I walked up to the corner and went into the bar where Curly sometimes went before dinner, but it was too early. I decided to wait. I ordered a vodka gimlet and got four because it was both ladies' day and happy hour. I drank two of them, and by the time I finished the second one I knew what I wanted to do.

I got up and left some money and took the T into Boston. I went straight to the Peace Corps offices, and explained my situation to a man in a suit. He was wearing a button that said "THE

NEW PEACE CORPS." This unnerved me since I wasn't sure if I had been in the old Peace Corps or the new Peace Corps, or what the difference was. When I had finished my story, he didn't say anything for a minute. We both just sat there.

Then he said, "You did resign, didn't you?"

"Yes," I said. "But it was a mistake. I want to withdraw my resignation."

"You can't," he said. "You have to reapply."

"But that's absurd," I said. "Can't I just go back?"

"No," he said. "This is all very complicated. You have to reapply, and then, if you are accepted, you'll have to be reassigned."

"I can't just go back to Slemba?"

"No," he said. "Why don't you take some time to think about this? It's probably just culture shock. It does take some time to readjust. Going back isn't always the solution."

"But I made a terrible mistake. I don't know why I didn't stay. I should have stayed."

"Why didn't you, then?"

"Well, I thought I wanted to come back and start a life here and a career and all that, but I've realized I don't."

"What?" he asked.

"Nothing," I said.

"The Peace Corps is not an escape. You can't use it to escape."

"I'm not escaping. That's why I want to go right back. If I stay here, I'll get another job or something, and that will be something to escape. But right now I don't have anything to escape from. Nothing. So it's not an escape." I thought this was a very good point, but the man just looked at me oddly.

"I'm sorry," he said. "I really think you should give this some time and thought. If you decide to reapply, I'll personally supervise your application and make sure it gets processed with the utmost expediency. But that's all I can do for you."

I took the application he handed me and went outside and sat in the plaza and started to fill it out, but halfway through, the pen

I had stolen from the receptionist's desk ran out of ink, but it ran out slowly, so the application was all scratched out and awful looking, and I started to cry. I hadn't cried once, during this whole ordeal, but once I started, I couldn't stop.

When I did stop crying, I realized my application now looked even worse: It was tear-stained and crumpled, so I tore it up and threw it away. I thought about going up and getting another application, but it was after five o'clock.

I must have sat there a long time because suddenly I realized it was getting dark. I thought about going back to Medford and trying to talk to Curly, but for some reason I knew it would be a waste of time. And I was sick of wasting my time. The plaza was starting to look ornery in the fading light, so I got up and tried to find a bus out to Pilgrim Acres. I figured I'd stay there for the night.

I wasn't planning on hitchhiking, but a car stopped beside me. "Need a ride?" the guy asked.

"Where are you going?"

"Out to Stockbridge," he said.

I got in the car. It seemed like the only thing to do. The man looked back over his shoulder, and pulled into the traffic. He didn't say anything for a minute. Then he looked over at me.

"Going to a party?" he asked.

I still had my Pilgrim costume on. "No," I said. "I work at Pilgrim Acres."

"Is that open nights?"

"Not usually," I said, "but tonight we're doing a special reenactment of the Battle of Gettysburg."

"Oh," the man said. "That sounds interesting."

"It's fascinating," I said. Then I realized he might want to come see it, so I added, "If you like that kind of thing. Most people find it really boring."

We drove a little further in silence. Then the man said, "I'm Drake. What's your name?"

"Clara," I said.

* * *

I told Drake to drop me at the exit because I knew if the guard saw the car drive up to the main gate, he would be suspicious. So I walked down the exit ramp and the mile out to Pilgrim Acres. The park was surrounded by a stockade fence topped with barbed wire, but I knew there was a gate by the cow field that was left unlocked. I had thought the cows would be put into a barn or something for the night, but they were still in the field. They were sitting under a tree, but as I walked across the field they stood up and watched me. They looked very ghostly in the moonlight: Their white patches shone like freshly spilled paint around the holes of their dark patches, and they swayed their big heads in a sleepy, curious way.

I climbed over the fence into the herb garden. Except for the cows, Pilgrim Acres was deserted. Even the swans in the swan pond had disappeared someplace. I walked up Main Street to the Bakery.

For a few minutes I just stood there; it looked so lovely, all shut up and quiet, the flowers in the window boxes curled tight for the night. But then I took out my keys and went in, locking the door behind me. I was afraid to turn on the lights in case the guard could see, so I lit a candle. There were two rocking chairs in the parlor, supposedly antiques. They had velvet ropes tied across their arms so tourists couldn't sit in them. I took the rope off one and sat down. I wondered who had sat there last—maybe a real Pilgrim.

I sat there and rocked, holding the candle. I watched it burn down, rocking the whole time.

THE NEAR FUTURE

"I think I should have got four," Natalie said.

We were standing in her spare bedroom looking at the throw pillows she had arranged across the back of the sofa bed. We had bought them at Ames on our way home from dropping my mother at the airport.

"What do you think?" Natalie said. "Don't you think it would look better if there were four? So there wasn't any space between?"

"I guess so," I said.

"Well, we'll just pick up another," Natalie said. She walked over to the bed and rearranged the pillows so they were lined up, touching one another. "That's good for now," she said. She sat on the bed, and patted the spot beside her. I went over and looked out the window. Dewey, Natalie's dog, was standing on top of his dog house, panting. He looked up at me.

"She must almost be there by now," Natalie said. "It only takes about three hours to fly to Dallas." She looked at her watch. "It must be real hot down there. When I was in Texas the road melted. They put up a road block 'cause cars were getting stuck. That's all I remember from Texas."

"Texas used to be the biggest state," I said. It was all I could think of to say.

Natalie stood up and rearranged the pillows, spreading them back out. "Are you O.K.?" she asked. She came over and stood behind me. Dewey was still watching me. He thought I was going to do something. He barked up at us. "That dog," Natalie said. "You'd think he'd be smart enough to stay out of the sun." She put her hands on my shoulders. She said, "This is all going to be just fine," and then she left me alone. She went outside and sprayed Dewey with the hose.

I had been living in the apartment downstairs with my mother, until she decided to move to Texas to marry a dentist she had met last winter at a dental convention. She had a job giving out free samples. She stole a lot. We still have miniature toothpaste tubes. She didn't tell the dentist she had a child; she promised me that when she got settled with him, she would tell him about me, and I could move down there if I wanted. In the meantime, I was renting Natalie's spare bedroom for fifty dollars a month, but I didn't have to start paying till I resumed my job at Ogermeir's Nursery. I had been laid off on account of the drought.

My mother waited until I was eighteen to move to Texas. This was so she couldn't be accused of abandoning me. How I know this is that she called in to a radio program with a lawyer. I just happened to be listening. She said her name was Beth. Hello, Dave, she said, I'm Beth. She asked her question. Beth, the lawyer said, you have no legal or financial obligation to an eighteen-year-old. In the eyes of the state, such a child is an adult.

When I was sixteen I stopped going to school. That's legal. I had been in special education. We didn't have a classroom—we met where they stored the paper. It looked like a closet but it wasn't. It was a storage room. Later we moved to a different room, but it wasn't special education anymore. It was called Headstart. The difference was, in Headstart we did things like putting things together. They didn't try to teach us things anymore.

* * *

A man named Hugo Trenti rented our old apartment downstairs. He slept during the day, because he worked at the pharmaceutical plant nights. He moved his bed down into the basement, where it was cool and dark, and put a sign on the front door that said "QUIET DAY SLEEPER."

Natalie worked at the college library. She was only supposed to work three days a week during the summer, but because it was air-conditioned, she went in every day. I went with her. I tore some things out of books but secretly. Just pictures. One night, on our way home, we stopped at Jamboree for burgers. Mr. Trenti was at the counter, eating scrambled eggs. Breakfast time for him.

"He's a perfect tenant," Natalie said. "He sleeps all day and is out all night."

"I wonder when he does things," I said.

"Maybe he just doesn't."

"He went to the races last weekend."

"How do you know?"

"He told me. He asked me to go with him."

"Maybe we'll all go to the races some night," Natalie said. "That could be fun." She looked over at Mr. Trenti.

"Do you have a crush on him?" I asked. A crush means you love someone till it hurts. I had a crush on Natalie.

"I'm too old for crushes," Natalie said. Natalie was divorced. When my mother and I first moved in, she was living with the chemist at Schnabel's, but about a year ago he was arrested for selling drugs. He was in prison upstate and once I went with Natalie to visit him. I stayed in the car while she went in, though. While I was waiting a woman came over and asked me to sign a petition for them to serve brewed coffee in the prison cafeteria.

Mr. Trenti got up, but instead of leaving, he went over to the jukebox. He read the list of songs all the way through before making his selection.

"Are you going to eat your pickle?" I asked Natalie.

She didn't answer. I could tell she was waiting to find out what song Mr. Trenti picked.

In Darcy, where we lived, you were allowed to water your lawn if you had your own well. In Chippenewa, where Ogermeir's Nursery was, it was against the law to water your lawn at all. You had to take showers at the high school; you could only flush your toilet once a day. When you drove out Route 91 to Chippenewa, you could tell when you crossed the boundary: It was like a tan line, only it was green and brown.

Mr. Trenti decided to grow a garden in the backyard. He asked me to help him. We dug up a square area of grass and then went down to Woolworth's and bought seeds. Mr. Trenti had a green pickup truck. There was a sticker on the bumper that said HIRE A VET. For a minute I thought animal doctor, then I remembered.

"Were you in Vietnam?" I asked him.

"Yes," Mr. Trenti said. He held out his arm. "See," he said.

"What?"

"It shakes," he said. "I have a permanent tremor."

It was hard to tell if it was shaking, because we were driving and everything was shaking a little. But when we got to the checkout at Woolworth's and Mr. Trenti looked through his wallet, I realized he was right: His arm did shake, like it needed to be tightened or something.

Mr. Ogermeir called me up and told me he had some work for me, despite the drought. I rode my bicycle out Route 91, which was soft and bubbling. My bicycle left a snake-like trail across the tar patches. Mr. Ogermeir was waiting for me. He was wearing his bathrobe. We went through the greenhouse and out the back. There were fields of baby Christmas trees, all of them dead. They were about three feet high, bright orange, and when I touched one the needles dropped off in clumps. My job was to dig them up and burn them. I was paid by the tree: twenty-five cents for every tree.

The next day I had to stay home because my arms were so badly scratched. I should have worn long sleeves. Mr. Ogermeir said I could come back when my skin healed.

No more watering of lawns in Darcy. Mr. Trenti and I had to abandon our garden. We decided to study for our high school equivalency diploma tests together. We'd move to Alaska and become forest rangers. At night before he went to work we sat on the front porch and asked each other questions from a workbook Mr. Trenti got from the VA:

> Name the thirteen original States.
> What's one-quarter times one-half?
> Who's Elizabeth Cady Stanton?
> Spell *chrysanthemum*.

Other things happened. Dewey stopped eating. Natalie and I took him to the vet. Dewey lay on the metal table, panting. White lather fell off his tongue. He eyed us all suspiciously.

"That's how dogs sweat," the vet said. "They can only sweat through their tongues."

He looked in Dewey's eyes and mouth; he took his temperature.

"What's the matter?" Natalie asked.

"It's just the heat," the vet said. "It's called heat fatigue. Dog days." He laughed. "Make sure he has plenty of water," he said. "Don't worry."

By the time my arms healed, Mr. Ogermeir had found somebody else to burn the Christmas trees. I got another job, painting fire hydrants. I walked from hydrant to hydrant, following a map I was given. When I ran out of red or silver paint, I used a citizen's telephone to call Town Maintenance. They sent a truck with more paint.

Some citizens were nice. They gave me drinks: beer or iced tea or lemonade. One lady gave me lunch, because the cheese sandwich I had brought with me melted to its plastic bag. One lady told me I could swim in her pool. As soon as I jumped in her dog jumped in, too.

"He's just trying to rescue you," the woman said.

The dog swam over to me and guided me, with its nose, to the side of the pool.

It got so hot we couldn't sleep. We didn't even try. Natalie and I sat outside, near the abandoned garden. The sky was full of stars, but the heat made them look out of focus. We drank beer, nice and slow, so we wouldn't get dizzy.

About four o'clock Mr. Trenti came home. We heard his truck in the driveway, and were illuminated in his headlights. He kept them on, watching us. Then he came and sat on the ground beside Natalie.

"It's hot," he said.

Natalie got him a beer. "It was hot once this way when I was little," she said. "People went crazy. At night my father took his gun out in the backyard and shot it up into the sky. Everyone was doing it. To relieve tension. Heat makes you tense."

"Don't let's talk about guns," Mr. Trenti said. "Or heat."

In the darkness I could see that Mr. Trenti had put his hand on top of Natalie's. She lifted her fingers and coiled them around Mr. Trenti's. They both kept staring straight ahead, as if it were their hands that were falling in love, not them. I got up and walked around front.

That afternoon I got a postcard from my mother. She was on her honeymoon in a place called Canyon Springs. She had learned to play badminton; things were going well. She said she hadn't mentioned me but she would. She was just waiting for the right moment. Sometime in the near future. The near future means soon. I wanted her to ask me to move to Texas so I could say no. I wanted to tell her I was moving to Alaska. Alaska is the biggest state now.

I crossed the street and walked behind the dry cleaner's. I stood in the middle of the gravel parking lot, throwing stones at the dark window, each throw harder, till the window broke. When the sound of it breaking was finished everything seemed especially quiet. I thought something might happen then, but it didn't.

After a while I heard a frog chirping down in the culvert, but when I walked toward it, it stopped. I stopped, too. Neither of us wanted to be the one to do something next.

THE MIDDLE OF EVERYTHING

Three days before his show opened, Jack arrived at his hotel in New York to find a telegram from his grandmother. He was not alarmed. His grandmother believed telegrams were the most civilized form of communication. This telegram, like all of hers, was succinct. It read: "Welcome New York. Awaiting your call." It was signed Mrs. Enid Winns Carter.

In his hotel room Jack was overcome with the paralysis he always felt upon arriving in New York. Lately he had made his home in Mexico, and occasionally, Los Angeles. He hadn't lived in New York City for nearly four years. He never knew where to begin in New York. He always felt as if he were coming in at the middle of everything.

He decided to begin by calling his grandmother. The phone barely rang once before she answered it. "Hello Grandma," Jack said.

"Hello," she said. "How are you?"

"I'm fine," he said. "A little jet-lagged."

"Who is this?" she asked. Mrs. Carter liked to act confused on the telephone. It was her least favorite form of communication.

"This is Jack," Jack said. Since he was her only grandchild, there could be little doubt as to his identity.

"Jack?"

"John," he said. "Your grandson."

"Oh, John!" she exclaimed. "It doesn't sound like you. Did you get my telegram?"

"Yes," he said. "How did you know where I'm staying?"

"Because you always stay at the same hotel. That horrible place downtown." He was staying at the Chelsea. A couple of years ago his grandmother had come into town to have lunch with him and had taken a taxi to the hotel. She refused to get out because she claimed Twenty-third Street looked like a circus. She took the taxi back up to the Sherry-Netherland, where she summoned him for a "civilized" lunch. Now Mrs. Carter avoided the city entirely.

"Can I expect you for dinner?" she continued.

"I should really check in at the gallery," he said.

"Couldn't you do that tomorrow?"

"I suppose," Jack said, who was none too eager to confront his paintings. They always looked inexplicably different and invariably worse in New York. "What time are the trains?" he asked. His grandmother lived in Bedford.

"I don't know," she said. "I haven't taken a train in ages. I suggest you call the train people. That's what they are for."

"I see you insist on looking like a field hand," Mrs. Enid Winns Carter said by way of a greeting. She was standing in the front hall, supported by a cane.

"You can't help getting at least a little tan when you live in Mexico," Jack said.

"Yes, but you could help living in Mexico." Mrs. Carter disapproved of North Americans living in foreign parts. She believed everyone should live where he was born. She had lived in the same house in Bedford since the 1920s. It was a large brick house with many rooms and much furniture. She led Jack, rather slowly, into the living room.

"Where is Aunt Helen?" he asked. His Aunt Helen, who was

really his grandmother's cousin, had lived with his grandmother for the last three years.

"Mrs. Whitcomb is drying out," his grandmother said. She always referred to Helen as Mrs. Whitcomb.

"Drying out?"

"She's at that clinic where you have to make your own bed. In California." She pronounced California with five syllables.

"I didn't know she had a drinking problem," Jack said.

"Of course she has," his grandmother said. "What do you think she has been devoted to all these years?"

"Nothing, I suppose," he said.

"Wrong," Mrs. Carter said. "She has been devoted to the bottle. And I don't understand this sudden urge to hop on the wagon. It seems a little late in the game."

"Better late than never," Jack said.

His grandmother snorted.

"How long will Helen be away?" Jack asked. He was worried about his grandmother living alone. She was eighty-six.

Mrs. Carter waved her hand. "Enough of Mrs. Whitcomb," she said. "I want to hear about you. Tell me about your show. Are the paintings big and ugly?"

"They're somewhat smaller this year," he said.

"But just as ugly?"

"You would think so," Jack said.

She smiled. "I still hope that before I die, you will paint me a nice picture. Would you begrudge me that?"

"I gave you the pick of the last show."

"No. I'm not interested in ugly paintings. I want a painting *of* something. I know that makes me hopelessly old-fashioned, but so be it. You know what I would most like? A painting of the house at Benders Bay. Surely you could paint that for me? After all your education and training, which I hasten to remind you I financed."

"I'll pay you back."

"Pay me with a painting of Benders Bay." Benders Bay was the house his grandmother once owned on Fishers Island. "I have a photograph of it, if you have forgotten what it looks like."

"I don't paint from photographs," Jack said.

"Then you could go out there and paint it. Although I wonder if it's still there. Perhaps it's been torn down."

"I doubt it," said Jack.

"Yet it's somebody else's now," his grandmother said. "Anyway," she continued, "I would like you to paint me something before I die."

"I'll go up to Fishers next week and paint you the house," he said.

"That makes me very happy," she said. "You have no idea."

Jack's grandfather had built Benders Bay as a wedding present for his wife. They had gone there every summer from 1923 to 1970, the year his grandfather died. Jack spent the summers at Benders with them. His father worked in the city, and his mother, a beautiful and not untalented actress, was usually in a show. She worked very steadily on Broadway during the '40s and the '50s. When Jack was fifteen she killed herself.

The summer weeks at Benders Bay always followed the same pattern: On Sunday, after the matinee, Jack's parents would arrive. His mother would bring an entourage—people from the cast, or other friends—and the house would be filled with exotic glamorous adults, with noise and music and cigarette smoke, with dancing and charades, with men and women running down to the water in the middle of the night, and reappearing, fully clothed, sopping wet, to dance some more. Then on Tuesday afternoon they'd pack everything up and depart in a caravan of honking cars for Manhattan, and an 8:30 curtain, leaving the elder Carters and Jack behind.

When his grandfather died it was revealed that he had several large debts, and his grandmother sold Benders to pay them. She never returned to Fishers Island.

*　　*　　*

"I am thinking of selling my accessories," Mrs. Carter said, as they ate dinner.

"What accessories?" Jack asked.

"Accessories," she said. "My gloves, and hats and jewels."

"Why are you going to sell them?"

"Why not?" his grandmother said. "Why keep them? Since you have disowned my great-grandchildren, there is no family to inherit them. And I am told there is an appreciative market for vintage accessories. I have spoken with several dealers."

"I haven't disowned the twins," Jack said. "I just don't have custody. There's a difference." Jack was the father of twin girls, Sigourney and Yvette. Shortly after they were born, he and his wife were divorced; Barbara immediately remarried, and his bitterness somehow poisoned his paternal love. Jack knew this was wrong, he knew that his feelings for these children should be separate from his feelings for their mother, but somehow they were all inextricably tangled, threads with many sharp needles, and he cast the whole net off and moved away.

"Call it what you will," Mrs. Carter said. "I never see them."

"Maybe I'm interested in your accessories."

"Why would you be interested in them?"

"I don't know. Perhaps I'll remarry. There's no need to sell them. You don't need the money."

"Are you contemplating remarriage?"

"No," he said.

"There is no one in your life?"

A vision of Langley, his lover, drying her hair with a white towel beside the aqua swimming pool, presented itself to him. He smiled. Why did he not want to tell his grandmother about Langley? It was probably her age—an unacceptable twenty-three—but he liked the fact that Langley was a secret, that she was unofficial, that she existed only in the palmy air of, as his grandmother would say, Californeea. "No one," he said, but the vision lingered.

"That is too bad. I wish you were in love. You are always a nicer person when you are in love."

"Isn't everyone?" he asked.

"No," said Mrs. Carter. "Love makes some of us villains. Come upstairs. I will show you my treasures. Whatever you want, you can take. The rest I will sell."

He followed his grandmother out of the dining room and into the front hall. Mrs. Carter had had an elevator chair installed along the banister, which was long and curved. She sat down and buckled a seat belt. "It won't go unless this is fastened," she explained. "Stupid thing." She pressed a button and the chair began to rise. Jack climbed the stairs next to her, one step at a time, trying to match her slow ascent. "For heaven's sake, walk normally," she said. "I'll meet you at the top."

On the second-floor landing he looked down and watched his grandmother rise. She was facing away from him, traveling backward, her hands clasped in her lap, her head bowed. That afternoon when he had driven her into town to buy groceries, she had sat the same way. Her loss of mobility was, in her eyes, a loss of dignity. The chair curved around and arrived at the top of the stairs; she unbuckled the belt and the chair tilted forward, depositing her next to him.

"This way," she said, all business in an attempt to transcend her humiliation. Jack followed her down the hall into her bedroom, then into her dressing room. She approached a large armoire that was made of either ash or pecan: some golden wood that was so highly polished they were both reflected in its veneer. It was dusk, and an imported, antique light filled the room. "Damn it," she said. "I forgot the keys. They're downstairs."

"Where are they? I'll get them."

"They're in my bag, in the front hall, on the credenza."

"I'll be right back."

When he returned with the ring of keys his grandmother was

sitting in an easy chair by the window. She held out her hand.

"Why do you keep it locked?" Jack asked.

"I keep everything locked," Mrs. Carter said. She flipped through the keys and found the one for the armoire. "Voilà," she said, handing it to Jack.

He opened the armoire. On the inner side of its doors were beveled mirrors mottled with green moss-like fog. One half of the space was a closet of dresses sheathed in dress bags. Sequins glinted, iridescent as crows' wings, in the darkness. The other half contained drawers of varying sizes. Jack opened one and found a stash of scarves, an unmade bed of glossy silk and lace. He felt his grandmother watching his back. The next drawer contained a jumble of gloves, an orgy of hands, gloves of every length and color, gloves with gauntlets, gloves with pearls and flowers and monograms embroidered on them. "Where did you get all this stuff?" he asked.

She snorted. "There was a time when people bought fine things and kept them."

He slid open a thin drawer. On a field of crimson velvet an army of brooches and earrings were pinned, all of them set with stones glittering in unembarrassed colors. "Are these real?" he asked.

Mrs. Carter didn't answer. She sat with a blank look on her face.

Jack closed the drawer. "Are you tired?" he asked.

She shook her head no. "I am thinking about your daughters," she said, looking out the window at the sun's disappearance.

"Oh," Jack said.

"Do they know they have a great-grandmother?"

"I don't think they remember you," he said.

"Of course they don't remember me. They haven't seen me since they were babies. My question was, do they know of me?"

"I think I've mentioned you," he said.

"Mentioned me? How generous of you."

"They are not a part of my life," Jack said.

"So you *have* disowned them." Mrs. Carter looked at him.

"No," he said. "You don't understand."

"Of course I don't understand, because your behavior is incomprehensible."

"They have a new father. I try not to interfere."

"How very gallant of you."

Jack closed the armoire and locked it. He played with the keys. They were old keys, made of iron. He wondered what else they opened. "I'm sorry," he said. "I wish things were different. I wish I were different."

For a moment neither of them said anything. Mrs. Carter looked back out the window. "I had to have the elm tree cut down," she said. "The town insisted on it. They said it was jeopardizing the electrical wires."

"That's a shame," Jack said.

She shrugged her thin shoulders. "They did a very neat job of it. All in a day."

"I didn't notice it was gone," said Jack.

"It's getting dark," said Mrs. Carter. "Turn on the light."

Jack's show was at the Winterburn Gallery, which was owned by a woman named Olivia de Havilland. She claimed this was her real name, and Jack saw no reason to doubt her, since there were a number of other equally odd things about her that were true. He spent an exhausting day hanging the show with her. She had the unfortunate idea that some of the canvases should be hung very high, and some very low, thus creating, in her words, "a dynamic viewing experience."

Although Jack had sent an invitation to the opening to his ex-wife, he was surprised to see her there. They usually avoided each other. But about halfway through the evening, Barbara entered the gallery, trailing a twin by either arm. The twins were dressed in brightly colored jogging suits; Barbara's newly restored body was tightly swathed in leather. She ignored the paintings and made right for Jack. "Greetings," she said, kissing the air beside his cheek. She indicated the twins and said, "les enfants," as though they were some exotic delicacy.

Jack didn't know what to do. He felt under-rehearsed. He was aware that everyone was watching him and that he was making a poor show. One of the twins—he had no idea which—clutched his leg. He reached down and patted her head. She looked up at him.

"Which one?" he said.

"Sigourney," Barbara said. "See Daddy's paintings," she said to the child. "Daddy painted these."

Sigourney studied a canvas that, thanks to Olivia de Havilland, was hung at her eye level. "I can do better than that," she said.

There was much tense laughter, followed by tense silence. Jack turned to Barbara. "How about dinner when this is over?" he asked.

"What's up?" asked Barbara.

"Nothing," said Jack. "I just thought it might be nice."

"With or without?" asked Barbara.

"With or without what?"

"Les enfants," said Barbara.

"Oh," said Jack. "With."

"If I'd known, I'd have brought the dog," Barbara said.

Barbara suggested a restaurant called Café Wisteria in Tribeca. The twins devoured a plate of cornichons and radishes and disappeared beneath the table. For a while Jack and Barbara concentrated on their food, and listened to the murmurings at their feet. Barbara was the most relaxed person Jack had ever met. Nothing seemed to faze her, which drove him crazy. The rumor was that she was addicted to Valium, but Jack knew for a fact that she wasn't. She just inhabited her life disinterestedly.

"How is Roger?" Jack asked. Roger was Barbara's new—well, not new anymore—second husband.

"Roger's fine. He's in Madrid at the moment. We're buying a house there."

"In Spain?"

"Outside of Barcelona."

"Why?"

"Why?" she repeated, as if she had never considered the question before. "I don't know. No reason, really. We plan to spend half the year there."

"Oh," Jack said. "You'll take the twins?"

"They're a little too young to fend for themselves."

"Of course," said Jack. "I just meant . . ."

"What?"

"I don't know. What will they do in Spain?"

"Learn Spanish, I hope. I don't know. What do they do in New York? Play. Grow up. Don't tell me you're developing an interest in them?"

Jack didn't say anything. A small hand was rolling his sock up and down his ankle. "Actually," he said, "I have been thinking about them. I was wondering if I could take them to visit my grandmother."

"How is she doing?"

"Well. She'd like to see the twins."

Barbara raised the tablecloth and addressed the floor. "Honeys," she said, "would you like to go visit your great-grandma? Jack wants to take you to Bedford."

"Where's Bedford?" a twin asked.

"Not far," said Barbara. "In the country. You get there on a train."

"Are there cows?"

"No, it's not a farm."

"Is there a trampoline?"

"No. Just a big house with your great-grandma, who wants to see you very much. And Jack will take you. Wouldn't that be fun?"

"Who's Jack?"

"You know Jack. Your father. Not Daddy, but your father." Jack leaned his head down and looked under the table. "It's me," he said. "I'm Jack." The twins looked up at him with identical, confused expressions on their small, perfect faces. "I'm Jack," he said again, and reached his hand down toward them, tentatively, as if to wild dogs.

At the hotel there was a message for him to call Langley Smith. Langley had originally been Jack's student, when he taught painting and lectured on modern art for one ill-fated semester at Bryn Mawr immediately following his exodus from New York. He had met her again, several years later, at the opening of a show of his in Los Angeles. By then she had switched from painting to acting. Her biggest claim to fame was as a guest star on "L.A. Law," playing a woman (unjustly) accused of child molestation.

"Hi baby," Langley said. "How did it go?"

"Not bad," Jack said. "Julian Arnotti bought the two big ones."

"Great," she said.

"How are you doing?" Jack asked.

"Not bad. I was called back again for the part in that pilot."

"What pilot?"

"The one for Lorimar. About the American family in Russia. You know, the dum-dum daddy's an ambassador, the ditsy mother's an alky, there are kids and a dog and a lot of funny commies."

"Who are you?"

"The daughter, if you can believe it. I'm a nympho with a thing for Ruskies in uniforms."

"That's great. And you got it?"

"Yes. Unless they decide to make the family black. As you

know, black is very popular out here now. They're negotiating with Richard Pryor, and if he says yes, then it will be black. But I doubt he will."

"Maybe you could be an adopted daughter. That would be interesting."

"I'll suggest it. So when are you coming back?"

"I don't know. In about a week. I'm a little worried about my grandmother."

"Why?"

"Well, my aunt who usually stays with her is drying out at Betty Ford. I don't think she should be living alone."

"Can't you get someone to stay with her? A nurse or someone?"

"I guess so. I'll have to look into it."

"If this Ruskie thing falls through maybe I'll fly out. It would be fun to spend some time in New York together."

"I don't know," he said. "I'm kind of preoccupied."

"You must be tired," Langley said. "What time is it there?"

"One o'clock."

"You want to go to bed?"

"Yes," he said.

"O.K., then. We'll talk later?"

"Sure," he said. "Listen, good luck with the thing. The pilot."

"Thanks," she said. "I'll let you know if I get it."

"Well, good night."

"Good night," Langley said. "I love you."

Jack hung up quickly, hoping his failure to respond to her declaration had gone unnoticed. But of course he knew it had not. And he had some idea of how Langley must feel: Langley, in her bedroom, the TV on, the sprinkler spraying the window; Langley in bed in her Tina the Killer Whale T-shirt, having said I love you to the miles between them, to the darkness, to his inevitable silence. She was better and braver than he, he understood that, but what he did not understand was why she tolerated his constipated dumb love, which he could express only when they lay down together and allowed their bodies to speak. He redialed the number of her house in Topanga Canyon. "Hello," he said. "C'est moi."

"Bonjour moi," Langley said. "What's up?"

"Nothing."

"Oh," said Langley.

"I miss you," he said, after a pause.

"I miss you, too," Langley answered.

"I'm a little drunk," he said.

"Go to bed," suggested Langley. "Sleep it off."

"I wish you were here," he said.

"So do I," said Langley.

"I really wish you were here," he said. "Really."

"I love you," said Langley.

He didn't answer. He just sat on his bed, the drapes drawn, the traffic in the street, the phone pressed to his ear.

"Sleep well," Langley said, and hung up.

While his grandmother and the twins had a tea party in the gazebo, Jack mowed the lawn. The gardener was in the hospital. Although he couldn't hear their conversation, which was obscured by the roar of the mower, he could tell they were having fun. Every time he trudged past the gazebo all three waved at him. His grandmother raised her teacup in salute.

The party was still in progress when he finished the lawn, but before he could join it his grandmother told him to shower and change. Jack still had clothes in the house, which he and his father had lived in from the time his mother had died till the time he went to college. His father died five years ago, of a heart attack while swimming in Long Island Sound.

Except to keep them clean, his grandmother had touched nothing in their bedrooms. His was the same as the day he had left for college, and his father's was the same as the day he went for his swim. Jack took a shower in the bathroom they had shared. There was still a bottle of his father's cologne in the medicine chest. He smelled it and then tentatively put some on his skin, but he didn't smell like his father. He stood naked in the cool bathroom and looked out across the lawn at his grandmother and his daughters in the backyard. They were putting on a show for one another. His grandmother stood up and sang "Getting to Know You." Then the twins performed a sort of tap dance, but without tap shoes or music it was rather thumpy and chaotic.

Jack watched from inside the house, like a voyeur.

He called his grandmother the next day. The phone rang and rang, unanswered. Fearing the worst, he took the first train to Bedford. The front door was unlocked. The curtains in the living room were all drawn and the house was dark. His grandmother lay on the sofa. She sat up as he entered the room.

"Who is it?" she asked, feeling on the coffee table for her glasses.

"It's me," he said, "John."

"Haven't you heard of knocking?" she asked.

"I thought something had happened to you," he said. "I tried to call you, and there was no answer. I thought you were dead."

"Not quite dead," she said. "Just napping."

"Jesus," he said. He opened the curtains.

"Close them," she said. "I'm trying to keep the house cool."

He closed the curtains and sat down beside her on the couch. He realized he was panting and tried to catch his breath. He was sweating, too. "Have you heard from Aunt Helen?" he finally asked. "When is she coming back?"

"Not for a while. Apparently she was moister than anyone of us thought."

"Well, I'm worried about you being here alone," Jack said. "I'm planning to go back home, and I don't like it that you're here alone."

"Actually," his grandmother said, "I was thinking about getting a chimpanzee."

"What?" he asked.

"A chimpanzee. For a companion. I've read they make wonderful companions. They're very intelligent, you know, and clean."

"Isn't it against the law to own wild animals?"

"Apparently not chimpanzees."

"I can't believe we're talking about monkeys. You aren't serious about this, are you?"

"Of course I am serious."

"I think it's sick. It's macabre. It's like Nora Desmond in *Sunset Boulevard*."

"Nor*ma* Desmond."

"Whatever."

"What about your promise?" Mrs. Carter asked.

"What?"

"I am changing the subject. You promised to paint me a picture of Benders Bay. I don't suppose you have."

Jack had forgotten all about the painting. "Oh," he said.

"You forgot? I thought so."

"I didn't forget. I just haven't had time. I've been very busy."

"Of course," she said.

"I'll go up this week," he said. "Before I go back."

Mrs. Carter leaned forward and kissed him. "It was very sweet of you to rush out here. I'm sorry I unplugged the phone. I should have told you. I keep it unplugged unless I want to make a call or expect one."

"What if someone has to get in touch with you?"

"They can send a telegram. That is what telegrams are for."

"Telegrams are delivered over the phone."

"What happened to the little men on bicycles?"

"I don't know. They all died."

This news momentarily silenced Mrs. Carter.

"Well, that's a shame," she finally said. "A damn shame." She stood up. "Come," she said. "It's lunchtime. Are you hungry? How about a sandwich?"

That night he called Langley. He explained about the painting, telling her he wasn't sure when he'd be back.

"That's very sweet of you, to do a painting for your grandmother," she said.

Jack let her think that. It was the second time that day someone had told him he was sweet, yet he felt less than sweet. "Did you get the part?" he asked.

"No," she said. "They're postponing production while they rethink the concept. They've decided it's politically incorrect to make fun of commies. I can't believe the end of the Cold War is fucking up my career."

"That's a shame," said Jack.

"That's the breaks," Langley said.

"Listen," he said. "Why don't you fly out here? And we'll go out to Fishers together? We can stay a couple of days."

"I don't think so," said Langley.

"Why not?" he asked.

"I don't know," she said. "I'm just, you know, going through a lot of stuff right now, and I want to get it sorted out."

"What stuff?"

"Just stuff. Life stuff, work stuff." She paused. "Love stuff."

"About me?"

"Bingo," Langley said.

"What's the problem?"

"Oh, I don't know," said Langley. "I don't even know that there is a problem. I'm just thinking about it."

"Well, can't you think about it on Fishers Island?"

"Baby, listen, call me when you get back to L.A. We'll talk about it then."

"You don't think we should talk about it now?"

"No. Have fun. Paint well."

"Wait," he said. "Don't hang up."

"What?" said Langley.

"Listen," he said.

"I'm listening," Langley said.

"I don't want to lose you," he said.

Langley didn't say anything.

"I don't want to lose you," he repeated.

"That's funny," Langley said.

"Why?"

Langley made a small noise that could either have been the beginning of a laugh or a sob.

"What's funny?" he asked.

"Nothing, really."

"Have I already lost you?"

"Maybe," Langley said. "A little."

"Listen, I'll come back tomorrow. I can paint the house later this summer."

"No," said Langley. "Paint it now. I told you I have stuff to think about. It's O.K. I'll be here when you come back."

"Well, don't think about anything till I get there."

"I'm a smart girl," Langley said. "I can't promise you that."

The next day Jack took a train to New London and rented a car and rode the ferry over to Fishers Island. He drove out to Benders Bay and parked at the end of the long, sandy driveway, and looked up at the house, which stood on a bluff above the water. It had not been changed. The lilacs were blooming. There was a strong breeze from the sea and it blew some lavender blossoms across the windshield. Jack closed his eyes. He could smell the lilacs and the salt water and the heat. He remembered a time when he and his grandmother had been playing Scrabble on the terrace. He could remember the same fragrant hot wind, and how every now and then they would have to lean forward, shelter the board, and place their hands over the intricately arranged tiles, so that their words would not blow away.

He got out of the car and assembled his easel and supplies at a point in the road where the house was best silhouetted against the sky. As he began drawing, a woman appeared on the terrace and looked down at him curiously. She began to walk down the driveway, and Jack thought of the questions she was bound to ask him—Who are you? What are you doing here? Why are you painting this house? He put down his piece of charcoal, and tried to think of some answers.

THE SECRET DOG

When my wife, Miranda, finally falls asleep, I get out of bed and stand for a moment in the darkness, making sure she won't awaken. Miranda is a sound sleeper: Life exhausts her. She lies in bed, her arms thrown back up over her head, someone floating down a river. I watch her for a moment and then I go downstairs to the closet where I keep my dog. On the door is a sign that says "Miranda: Keep Out."

Miranda is allergic to dogs, and will not allow them in the house. So I have a secret dog.

I open the door to the closet without turning on any lights. Dog is sleeping and wakes up when she hears me. I have trained her to sleep all day and never to bark. She is very smart. In fact she is remarkable. I kneel in the hall, and Dog walks over and presses her head into my stomach. I hold it gently. The only sound is Dog's tail wagging, but it is a very quiet sound, and I know it will not wake Miranda. This is a moment I look forward to all day.

Dog and I go out to the car. I purposely park down the street so Miranda won't hear the car start. I tell her I can never find a space in front of the house. She suspects nothing. Once Dog and I are in the car, I feed her. I keep her food in the glove compartment. I keep the glove compartment locked. Dog stands on the front seat next to me and eats her dinner. I stroke her back while she is eating. Every few bites she looks up and smiles at me.

When she is done eating I start the car. I drive about a mile to an A&P that is open all night. As I drive, Dog stands with her nose out the window. I open the window only a crack because I am afraid Dog might jump out.

At the A&P we get out. First I take her behind the store to a grassy bank beside the railroad tracks where she can relieve herself. Every few days she does this in the closet, but usually she is very good about waiting till we get out. She hops about the tracks, sniffing and wagging her tail. She is a joy to watch. She squats, and I look the other way.

Then we go back to the parking lot, which is usually empty. Every now and then a car pulls in and someone jumps out and runs into the A&P. We have plenty of room. This is when I train Dog. I have a book, which I also keep locked in the glove compartment, called *How to Train Your Schnauzer*. Dog is not a schnauzer, but it seems to be working well. We are on week nine, although we've only been working for four weeks. That is how smart Dog is.

I have to give Dog plenty of exercise so she will sleep all day. We begin running. Dog runs right beside me. We run a mile or two through the deserted streets of the sleeping town and then walk back to the car. Dog trots beside me, panting. Her long pink tongue hangs out one side of her mouth. She stops and sniffs at discarded papers that flutter on the sidewalk.

We do this every night.

One night when I come in, there is a light on in the kitchen. This has never happened before. I put Dog in her closet and quietly close the door. I walk slowly up to the kitchen. Miranda is standing by the table in her bathrobe. She is slicing a banana into a bowl of cereal. She won't look at me. Her hair is loose and hangs down over her face, which is bowed above the banana. I cannot see her face. I sit down and still she will not look at me. Miranda,

I often think, looks more beautiful when wakened from sleep than during the day.

Suddenly the knife slits her finger, but Miranda does not acknowledge this wound. She continues to slice the banana. I realize she is crying.

"You cut yourself," I say, quietly. I think I can hear Dog plopping down on the floor in the closet.

Miranda raises her cut finger to her mouth. She sucks on it, then wraps it in a napkin. She tucks her hair behind her ears and sits down. Then she looks up at me. "Where have you been?" she whispers. There are two pink spots, high on her white cheeks. There is also a little blood on her lips. She has stopped crying. "Where have you been?" she repeats.

I watch the napkin she wrapped her finger in turn red, slowly. I cannot speak. Miranda stands up. She runs her finger under the faucet, and looks at it. She wraps it in a clean napkin. She is facing away from me, toward the sink. "Who are you seeing?" she says. "Do I know her?"

It has never occurred to me that Miranda might think I am having an affair. This is a great relief, for if she believes this she must not suspect Dog. "I'm not having an affair," I say. "I haven't seen anyone."

Miranda looks over at me. "Really?" she says.

"Yes," I say. "Really."

"Where have you been?" asks Miranda.

I think for a moment. "I can't tell you."

Miranda looks down at her injured finger. "Why can't you tell me?"

"It's a secret," I say. "I can't tell you because it's a secret. But I'm not having an affair. Do you understand?"

For a few seconds Miranda says nothing. She glances above my head at her reflection in the window. I, too, turn and watch her in the window. She looks very beautiful. I see her mouth move against the night. "Yes," she says. "I understand."

*   *   *

The next day at work I find I am very tired. I have been sleeping very little since I got Dog. Suddenly I wake up. Joyce, my boss, is standing in front of my desk. She smiles at me. "You've been sleeping," she says. "That isn't allowed."

I sit up straight and open my top desk drawer as if I'm looking for something. Then I close it. I look up at Joyce. She just stands there. "Why are you sleeping?" she asks. "Are you tired?"

"I'm exhausted," I say.

"Why?" asks Joyce.

"My wife just had a baby," I lie. "It's been very sick, and I have to stay up all night with it. That's why I'm tired." This is a very bad lie. Miranda and I can't have a baby.

"When did Miranda have a baby?" Joyce smiles. She sits down in my customer chair. "I didn't even know she was pregnant."

"A month ago," I say. "I thought I told you. I guess I've been too tired."

"How wonderful!" says Joyce. "Lucky you! What is it?"

"What do you mean?" I say.

"A boy or a girl?" asks Joyce. She is so nice.

"It's a girl."

"What's her name?"

I think for a second. "Dorothy," I say.

"Well," says Joyce, "congratulations." She stands up, and winks at me. "Just try to stay awake," she says. "But I understand."

The next night when I get home there is a big bouquet on the kitchen table. Miranda is sitting at the table, smoking. Miranda quit smoking years ago, although sometimes I find a pack beneath the seat of the car. What I do then is take them all out but one. I leave one for her to smoke, and toss the rest.

Miranda points to the flowers with her cigarette. Then she hands me a little card. A stork flies across the top, carrying a baby wrapped in a diaper. Pink ribbons form the words "Congratulations on the New Arrival!" and underneath that is written "Welcome Dorothy! Love, Joyce." The *o* in Joyce contains two little eyes and a big smile.

Miranda stubs her cigarette in the ashtray. "Who," she says, "is Dorothy?"

"I don't know," I say.

"If this is Joyce's idea of a joke," cries Miranda, "I think she must be pretty sick." She stands up and looks at the flowers. They are irises and tulips and a shriveled pink balloon on a stick. Miranda popped the balloon. Maybe she did it with her cigarette. "She must be pretty sick," Miranda repeats. "Since when do we have a baby? Did you tell Joyce we had a baby?" Miranda looks at me. "Did you?"

I don't know what to say. I never thought Joyce would send us flowers. I didn't think she was that nice. "Yes," I say, finally.

"You did?" Miranda is screaming, and it occurs to me that she is probably hysterical. "How could you? Why?"

"I fell asleep at work," I say. "It was just an excuse. I told Joyce I had to stay up nights with our baby. With Dorothy. I said Dorothy was very sick and I had to stay up nights with her."

"You're awful," says Miranda. "You're a moron. I don't understand what's happened to you. What's happened to you? I bet you are having an affair."

"Calm down," I say. "That's not true. You know that's not true. You said you understood. Remember?"

"But I don't understand," says Miranda. "I don't understand anymore. Where do you go at night?"

"It's a secret," I say. "I told you it was a secret."

"You can't have a secret like that," says Miranda. "I can't— Why can't you tell me? What could be so bad that you couldn't tell me?"

"It isn't bad," I say.

"Then why can't you tell me?"

"It's just private," I say.

"But I'm your wife," says Miranda.

"I know you're my wife," I say. "I love you."

"Do you?" asks Miranda.

"Yes," I say.

"And you don't love someone else?"

Dog isn't really a someone. She's a something. I love something else. I love Dog and I love Miranda. If Miranda weren't allergic it would all be fine. "No," I say.

Miranda stands up. "I'm going to bed," she says. "I don't feel well." She walks past me, toward the door, then she turns around. "Please get rid of the flowers," she says.

That night I wait a long time before I go down to Dog. I want to make sure Miranda is fast asleep. Finally I am satisfied. Miranda's face is turned away from mine on the pillow and her cheeks move in and out a little and the blankets rise and fall across her breasts, but besides that she is perfectly still. The lights from passing cars flit across her face, and she almost looks dead, she is so still.

I go down to get Dog. It is wonderful to see her. She comes out of the closet and whines a little, very quietly. Then she rubs her head against my chest. I am very sad tonight, and even Dog cannot cheer me up. Patting her, kissing her between her eyes, only makes me sadder. Dog senses this, and lies down close beside me on the car seat.

At the A&P I almost lose Dog. She runs between two huge trucks that are parked behind the store, and disappears. It is dark back here and quiet. There is no one about. I think I can hear Dog's tags and collar jingling, but it sounds very far away, on the other side of the tracks. I am afraid to call her, it is so quiet. The moon is out and broken glass glints on the pavement. I whistle softly, and finally Dog comes. I hear her coming across the tracks and back between the trucks. She runs across the parking lot, in and out of the shadows, like a ghost. I put out my hand to touch her, and she is there.

I go into the A&P to buy dog food. Dog is afraid of the automatic door and shies when it swings open of its own accord. I pick her up.

"You can't bring the dog in here," says the checkout girl. "Unless he's a Seeing Eye dog. Are you blind?"

Since I am carrying Dog, I can hardly claim I am blind. "No," I say. I put Dog down.

"Well, then he can't come in. Sorry."

I pick up Dog and go back out. Dog is tired; her body is limp and warm in my arms. I carry her like a baby, her head against my shoulder. I put her in the car, lock the door, and go back in the store.

I walk up and down the aisles enjoying myself. Pet food is always in the middle aisle, regardless of the store. This fact fascinates me. The only other person in the store is in pet food. She's wearing a long green dress, sandals, and a pink scarf. Her red hair sticks out from under the scarf in all directions. She stares at me as I walk down the aisle. She is waiting to tell me something, I can tell.

"I read palms," she whispers, as I reach out for the dog food. "I tell fortunes."

I say nothing. I read the box. "Complete as a meal in a can," it says. "Without any of the mess."

"Do me a favor," the woman says. She reaches out and touches my arm.

"What?" I say.

"Escort me up and down the aisles," she says. "I'll read your palm when we're done."

"Why?" I say.

"Why what?" Before I can answer she says, "Why not? I'm lonely. Please."

"O.K.," I say. I hope this won't take too long.

We walk toward the front of the store. The woman consults her shopping list. "My name is Jane," she says, as if this is written on her list. "Just Jane. Soda. Will you do me another favor?" She looks up at me.

"What?" I say.

She touches my arm again. "Pretend you're my husband," she says. "Pretend we're married and we're shopping. Will you do that?"

"Why?" I ask.

Once again she looks at her list, as if the answer is there. "Soda," she mumbles. "What kind of soda do you like?" She hesitates. "Dear."

We are in the beverage aisle, and all the bottles gleam around us. "I like Seven-Up," I say, because that is the first kind I see.

"The un-cola," says Jane. "I don't like it. I like Coke. But we'll get Seven-Up for you." She puts a large plastic bottle of Seven-Up in the cart. We proceed.

"Please don't get that for me." I feel very foolish. "If you like Coke, get Coke. I like Coke fine."

She stops. "Do you?" she says. "Do you like Coke fine?"

"Yes."

"But which do you like better?"

"Please get whatever you want," I say. "This is silly."

Jane puts the Seven-Up back on the wrong shelf. "Do you like birch beer?" she asks.

"Yes," I say.

"Fine, then." Jane reaches for some birch beer. "We'll get that."

We continue through the store like this, disagreeing about yogurt, deodorant, bread, juice, and ice cream. The checkout girl rings up my dog food first. Then she does Jane's groceries. I help her carry them out to her car. It is the only other one in the parking lot. I can see Dog, with her front paws poised on the dashboard, watching me. "Good night," I say to Jane. I'm glad this is over.

"Wait," says Jane. "I promised to tell your fortune. Give me your palm."

I hold out my hand and Jane takes it. Her hand is warm and wet. "Move." She pushes me back toward my car, under the light. She opens my palm and holds it flat. She wipes it off with her scarf. The light makes it look very white. For a long time she says nothing. I can hear Dog whine in the car.

When Jane speaks, she addresses my palm and not me. "I see blue lights. I see swimmers. I see rhododendrons. You will live a long time." She pauses. "You will always feel like this." She slowly rolls my fingers toward my palm, making a fist. She looks up at me.

"Like what?" I ask.

Jane lets go of my hand, and makes a vague gesture with her own, indicating the A&P, the parking lot, my car with Dog in it. "Like this," she repeats, softly. "You will always feel like this."

Joyce is there, standing above me. "Perhaps you should take some sick time," she says. "You can't keep falling asleep at work."

I feel very tired. I just want to go back to sleep. I don't know what to say.

"Do you have any comp time coming?" says Joyce. "Perhaps you should take it now."

"I'm tired," I say. Joyce is a little out of focus, on account of I just woke up.

"I know you're tired," says Joyce. She seems to be talking very loudly. Joyce sent us flowers. She is nice. "You look very tired. That's why I think you should take some time off. Don't you think that would be a good idea? Do you understand?"

"I guess so," I say.

"Well, think about it," says Joyce. "Think about it, and let me know. Things can't go on like this."

"I know," I say.

"Good," says Joyce. Then she leaves.

When I get home that night things are fine. Miranda suggests we go out to dinner, and we do. It is very nice. We drink a lot of wine and eat and eat and then we drive home. We watch the news on TV. It is terrible news; even the local news is terrible. Miranda yawns and goes into the bathroom. I can hear her in there: the water flowing, the toilet flushing. It all sounds so lovely, so safe. I can hear Miranda setting the alarm in the bedroom, and the radio playing softly.

"Are you coming?" she calls down the hall. "Come to bed."

I get in bed with Miranda and pretend to go to sleep. It is windy and cold outside, and the trees rattle against the windows. It is hard to stay awake. My head is spinning with all the wine I drank, and I am so tired. But I stay awake until Miranda falls asleep. I get up and go down to Dog.

When I open the closet, Dog is not there. The closet is empty. I call Dog softly, thinking she has got out somehow. I call and call, in little whispers, but she doesn't come.

I stand in the hall for a long while thinking I must have fallen asleep. Maybe I am dreaming. I do not understand what is happening, and I begin to cry a little. I go back upstairs and into the bathroom and close the door. When I stop crying I come out and stand in the bedroom. Moonlight falls through the window and onto the bed; onto the part where I am not sleeping, onto the empty spot beside Miranda, who sleeps against the wall, in shadow. The first time I saw Miranda was in a hotel in Florida. She was coming out of her room with a folding beach chair. She asked me to hold it while she answered the telephone, which was ringing in her room. I stood in the corridor and held the chair for what seemed to be a very long time. I could hear Miranda talking in her room, but I couldn't make out what she was saying.

Miranda wakes up. She turns over, into the moonlight, and looks up at me. "What are you doing?" she says, sleepily. "Why aren't you in bed? Are you crying?"

I realize I am still crying a little. Miranda sits up in bed, very beautiful, the light pale on her face. "Why are you crying?" she asks.

I don't know what to say. The wind blows and the bedroom seems to shake. I can hardly speak. "Where is Dog?" I finally say. "What did you do with Dog?"

"Dog?" says Miranda. "What dog?" She leans forward, across the bed, toward me.

THE CAFÉ HYSTERIA

A few days before Christmas I come home from work to find my friend David sitting on the little red velvet banquette in my mirrored lobby.

"Hi, Lillian," he says.

"Hi," I say. "What are you doing here?"

David stands up and kisses me. "Just hanging out," he says. "No. I came to give you this." He hands me a Christmas present: a tiny gift-wrapped box.

"This is for me?" I ask.

"No," David says. "It's for your mother."

"Come on up," I say.

We get in the elevator along with a woman in a fur coat. When she gets off on the fourth floor David says, "Merry Christmas." She doesn't answer him.

"You have a very unfriendly building. I said 'Merry Christmas' to everyone who came in your lobby while I was waiting. Only about three people answered me."

My apartment is pretty clean except for a half-eaten cinnamon Pop-Tart on the coffee table. While David hangs up his coat I hide it under a *Time* magazine.

David sits on the couch. "I think I'm a little drunk," he says. "We had our office Christmas party today. It was awful."

"Do you want some wine? Or a drink?"

"I better not," David says. "But I will. Just some wine. Or a beer. Do you have a beer?"

"No," I say.

"Then wine."

I go into the kitchen. David follows with the present. "Open this," he says. "I'll get the wine."

I exchange the corkscrew for the present. "Since when do you give me Christmas presents?"

"I don't know," David says. "Since now. Open it."

I open the present. David watches me, a glass of wine in either hand. Inside the box is a thin silver ring set with five small rubies. It's an old ring; I've seen it before. When Loren married David, his mother gave her three of them. There was one with diamonds and one with sapphires. She wore all three of them stacked on one of her long fingers. Loren and David are divorced now. Loren is, I suppose, my best friend.

"Isn't this Loren's?" I ask.

"No," David says. "Not anymore."

"But why are you giving it to me? You should give it back to your mother. Or save it for Kate."

"There are others. Kate can have the others. I wanted you to have this one."

"Why?" I ask.

David puts the glasses of wine down on the table. "I don't know," he says. "I feel bad. I mean, I know how you feel."

"About what?"

"Me," David says.

I put the lid on the box and hand it to David. "Here," I say. "I'm sorry but I can't accept it."

"Why can't you accept it?"

"I don't want it," I say. "You shouldn't have given it to me." I drink some of my wine.

David opens the box and looks at the ring. He touches it with his finger. "You don't understand," he says. "It's no big deal. It's just a token. Of affection. I want you to have it. It's important to me that you do. Please?"

He holds out the box. I sip my wine. I decide I'll take the ring for David's sake. If he wants to give it to me so badly, O.K. But I won't ever wear it and I won't ever let it mean anything to me. It will just be this ring.

"O.K.," I say. "Thanks."

"Put it on," David says. "Try it on."

I take the ring out of the box and put it on my right-hand ring finger. "See," I say, laying my hand flat on the table.

David touches my hand. "It's beautiful," he says.

"I'll be right back," I say. I go into the bathroom. I wash my face, and rinse it with cold water. When I come out David is standing in the living room eating the Pop-Tart.

"I'm starving," he says. "Do you want to go out to dinner? Or are you doing something?"

"Where do you want to go?"

"Well, actually, I was thinking about going downtown. To the place where Heath works." Heath is David's lover. He was David's temporary secretary last summer when his real secretary went on vacation.

"He's not at the bank anymore?"

"He hasn't been for a while. He's a waiter, at this place called Café Wisteria. Do you want to go? It's supposed to be good. Come. It will be fun."

Café Wisteria is a large, noisy restaurant. There are several dozen decorated Christmas trees hanging upside down from the ceiling. David confers with the hostess, a black woman in a green leotard.

"See," David says, as we sit down. "I told you this would be fun."

I try to locate Heath in the whirling mass of waiters, busboys, and diners, but it's hard because all the waiters look alike in that gay–New York waiter way. They're all tall and handsome. They all look like they just got their hair cut: The backs of their heads are as smooth and tended as their faces.

"Which one is Heath?" I ask. I have to yell over the music.

"I don't see him," David shouts back. A waiter who looks very much like Heath but who isn't Heath comes to take our drink order. Moments later they arrive, along with a plate of crudités shaped like a wreath.

David and I don't talk much; we eat broccoli and watch the crowd. Now Ella Fitzgerald is singing "Santa Claus Is Coming to Town," and as I sip my cold amber drink I think she's wrong, he's already come, he's here. I feel like we're sitting on the ceiling, or we're falling, or the trees are falling. Something's falling.

"What are you doing for Christmas?" David asks.

"Going to my parents'," I say. "It will be deadly. Julian's in South America and Adrian is going on this lesbian cruise to the Greek Islands. So it will be just me and Harriet and Winston."

"Christmas is the worst," David says. "It's designed to make people like us feel bad."

"What are you doing?"

"Actually, it might work out O.K. for me this year. I have Kate Christmas Eve and Loren has her Christmas day. Gregory is going to be in L.A., so instead of shuffling her back and forth, Loren and I will take her up to my mother's. We'll pretend we're still married for a few days."

"Does Gregory know?"

"I don't know," David says. "I take it things are kind of rocky with them."

"What about Heath?"

"I can't very well take Heath to my mother's," David says. "Not that he'd come. Not that I'd ask him."

"Does your mother know about Heath?"

"God, no. My mother is still waiting for me to get back together with Loren. She wants a grandson."

"My mother has given up on us producing natural grandchildren," I say. "She's joined this program called 'Guardian Grandparents.' She's adopted about eight million black children. She's always showing me pictures. It's cruel."

David isn't listening. And then I see why: He's watching Heath approach through the crowd of tables, turning sideways to let people pass.

I love eating out. It makes me feel sexy and wanted. I know that everyone in this restaurant—except Heath—assumes David and I are lovers. It's just something you assume about people who are eating together. If you see a man and a woman walking down the street you don't assume they're lovers, because walking down the street isn't sexy. But if you see the same two people in a restaurant, it's different. It is sexy. It's great.

I look around the huge room at all the people leaning toward one another across the lavender tablecloths, their faces glowing with candlelight and quiet erotic energy, but then I realize that all these other couples, people who look like they can't wait to get home and fall into bed with each other—maybe they're all just like David and me. Maybe there's nothing really happening between them, maybe it's just the wine and the food and music. Maybe nobody's getting what they want anymore, maybe everything is complex and involved, and everyone here will go home alone to their cats and clock radios.

Heath arrives, with a second round of drinks. "Hi," he says. "Welcome to Café Hysteria." He puts his hand on David's shoulder. "Are you guys having fun?"

"It's great," I say.

"The drinks are on the house," Heath says. "But you have to pay for the food."

"What should we order?" David asks.

"The swordfish isn't bad. Avoid anything with sauce. The sauce chef didn't show up. They're trying to wing it back there."

*   *   *

Heath gets off work early and joins us for coffee. He's changed into his street clothes and it looks like he might have taken a shower. He smells very clean, and his hair looks wet, although it could just be slicked back with stuff.

The three of us have trouble talking. We talk about the dinner—it was good; then about what Heath's doing for Christmas—he's working. I excuse myself and go to the ladies' room.

There's a woman leaning against the sink smoking, and she's still there when I come out of the stall. She's wearing a gold lamé space suit. "Did you happen to see this guy out there?" she asks. "He's wearing sunglasses and has a funny nose?"

"How funny?"

"I don't know," she says. "It's too big or something."

"I don't think so," I say.

"Could you check. Please?"

I open the door. There's a man standing at the telephone watching the ladies' room. He's wearing shades and his nose is funny looking. I close the door.

"He's out there," I say. "He's on the phone."

"He's been on the fucking phone for hours," the woman says.

"Who is he?"

"Oh, just some noxious freak of nature I used to be married to. He follows me around and verbally abuses me. Could you do me a favor?"

"What?"

"Just walk out with me, and talk. He'll leave me alone if I'm talking to someone. He's a coward."

"O.K.," I say. "Sure."

We walk out of the ladies' room. The man hangs up the phone and shouts "Julie! Julie!"

"Walk," Julie urges. "Just keep walking."

I escort Julie safely to her table. She is dining with a large group of similarly outfitted people. She promises to do the same for me someday.

I return to my table. "We're going over to Heath's," David says. "*It's a Wonderful Life* is on TV. Do you want to come?"

"No," I say. "I'll just go home."

"Come," says Heath. "It'll be fun. Besides, you've never seen my apartment."

This hardly seems like reason enough to go, but I don't argue this point. I'm sick of resisting things.

The cab drops us off at the corner of Twentieth Street and First Avenue. David goes into a Korean market to buy coffee beans and cigarettes.

Heath and I go up to his apartment. It's right over the little store. There's a large open room which has a kitchen at one end. There's a fat cat sleeping on the kitchen table. Along one whole wall is a floor-to-ceiling mirror.

Heath picks up the cat. "This is Spike," he says.

"What are the mirrors for?" I ask.

"My roommate is a dancer," says Heath. He hangs our coats up.

"I didn't know you had a roommate," I say.

"He's on tour," Heath says. "He's not around very much. He's with Alvin Ailey."

He turns the TV on. Jimmy Stewart is crying and praying in a bar. We both watch. After a few minutes David comes in. He must have keys. He's bought espresso beans, a pint of Häagen-Dazs ice cream, and a pack of Marlboro Lights.

Heath gets up and grinds the beans. I pretend to be very interested in the movie. Now Jimmy Stewart is driving his car into a tree. Suddenly the room smells of coffee.

We drink espresso and watch the movie. Heath and David sit on the couch, and I sit on a chair. After a while I get up and use Heath's bathroom. It is wallpapered with postcards. There's one, right above the light switch, of Block Island that I'm sure David sent him. David's mother has a house on Block Island. I went there once with Loren and David, when they were still married. I untack the card and turn it over. It is from David.

Dear Heath,

The weather has been great and I'm having fun. Today I played golf with my brother. Do you play golf? It's boring, I think. Hope you had a good weekend.

Regards, D.

I tack it back up. Regards, I think: not love.

When I go back into the living room someone has turned the lights off so just the TV illuminates the room. David and Heath are sitting close together on the couch, passing the pint of Chocolate Chocolate Chip ice cream back and forth. I watch them for a minute, from behind.

I hate being here. I put on my coat. They don't hear me. I have a feeling Heath is stroking David's leg but I can't really see. I could be just imagining it.

"I'm going to go," I say. "Thanks for the espresso."

They both turn around.

"Don't leave yet," Heath says. "It's almost over."

"I've seen it before," I say. "Many times."

"Lillian, wait," David says. "I was going to go back uptown with you."

I don't believe this for a second. David has no intention of going back uptown. If you're going back uptown you don't take your shoes off.

"I want to leave now," I say. "I'm tired."

"How are you going to get home?" David asks.

"Cab it," I say. I put my gloves on.

"Can I come down and help you find one?"

"That's all right," I say. They both finally get up off the couch and come over to the door. "Good night," I say.

Before they can kiss me I leave. When I get out on the street I look back up at the apartment window. I can't see them—just the silvery light from the TV. I go into the little store and buy a pack of cigarettes. A middle-aged Asian man in a jacket and tie sells them to me. He is very kind. He gives me three packs of matches and wishes me Merry Christmas. I feel like hanging out with him for a while. Like the rest of my life.

Instead, I start walking up First Avenue. It's warm out and the fresh air feels good. Across the intersection of First Avenue and Thirty-fourth Street, Santa is flying in a reindeer-pulled sleigh. The reindeer diminish in size: Each one is smaller than the one behind it. It's supposed to look like they're flying away into the night, but it doesn't. It looks like Santa couldn't find enough healthy reindeer this year. I take off my gloves to smoke a cigarette, and notice the ring on my finger. I forgot I had it on. I think of ways to get rid of it: tossing it under the wheels of a bus or handing it to a bum. I don't do either of these things, though. I just stand under a streetlight and look at it.

NOT THE POINT

The halls of the high school are teeming with manic, barely dressed students, and I press myself against the tile wall and let them pass. There is something frighteningly erotic about this sea of bodies: Girls' stomachs and boys' shoulders are bared in a combination of what seems to be narcissism and lust, as if they have emerged, not from History, but from some orgy, and are roaming the corridors in an effort to regroup, return to their lairs, and continue doing whatever it is they do behind these steamy glass doors.

After a few minutes, a bell shrills, the halls clear, and the school regains its composure. I find my way to the guidance office, and Mrs. King, Ellery's counselor. She asks me to sit down.

"Mr. Groener couldn't come?"

"No," I say. "He's in the Philippines."

"Philadelphia?"

"No, the Philippines."

"The Philippines?"

"On business."

"Of course," says Mrs. King, as if I were lying. "Well, I've taken the liberty of asking the school nurse to join us. I hope that's all right with you?"

I nod.

"Ellery's problems—or troubles—are not only academic. That's why Mr. Katikonas wanted to speak with us."

"Who's Mr. Katikonas?"

"Oh, he's the nurse. Miss Holloran retired, and, in an effort to update our health offerings, we've hired Mr. Katikonas. He has a background in drug and alcohol abuse, as well as adolescent psychology. Educational nursing has changed since our day." Mrs. King pauses, and then adds, "Not that Ellery's problems are stimulus-effected."

I smile.

Mr. Katikonas enters the small cubicle. He is wearing jeans and a T-shirt that says "Say No" on its chest. If I had met him in the hall I would have thought he was a student. He shakes hands with me, and then with Mrs. King, as if he knows each of us equally poorly. Perhaps he does. He looks around for a chair, but there isn't one.

"Oh," says Mrs. King. "You can get a chair from Willy's office."

"That's O.K.," says the nurse. "I'd rather stand." He leans against the wall.

"Well," says Mrs. King, "Mr. Katikonas and I wanted to talk to you about Ellery. Mainly about the sunglasses."

"I guessed," I say.

"You're aware of the problem?" Mrs. King asks.

"Yes."

"So he wears them at home?" the nurse asks. I pause, think about lying. But I don't. "Yes," I say.

"All the time?"

"Yes."

"Do you have any idea why?"

"No."

"Have you talked to him about them?" Mrs. King is obviously our group leader.

"A little," I say.

"And what did he say?"

"Nothing, really," I say. "I mean, I just kind of kidded him . . . I didn't want to make a big deal out of it."

"He could be doing serious retinal damage," the nurse interjects.

"Oh . . ." I say.

"I'm sure that's true, John, but that's not the point," says Mrs. King. "I think the glasses are a psychological shield he's building up around himself . . . they're a symbol for a deeper problem. The problem isn't really the sunglasses."

"Nevertheless," says the nurse, "he could be damaging his eyes. I feel it's important to make that point. From a health point of view."

"Thank you," I say.

"Mrs. Groener?" Mrs. King asks.

"Yes," I say.

"Could this be linked with . . . I mean, Ellery's record mentions his brother's recent death. Since he's a new student, I'm afraid I don't know him as well as some of my other students. But do you think this is linked with that?"

Ellery's twin brother, Patrick, committed suicide last year. We're still trying to adjust, I think. We moved to this new town, and now we're getting ready to move to the Philippines, where my husband's been transferred (at his own request). I don't answer. I don't yet know how to answer questions like these.

"Excuse me," Mrs. King says.

"No," I say. "It's O.K. I just really don't know."

"Of course," she says. "To return to the matter at hand. This school has no specific policy regarding the wearing of sunglasses. However, we do forbid the wearing of clothes and accessories that are either dangerous or that divert attention from the purpose of education. I think the sunglasses could fall into either of those categories."

"Yes," I say. "I suppose they could."

"So we're thinking of forbidding Ellery to wear them in the building."

"But I thought the problem wasn't the sunglasses," I say.

"But it's the . . . the manifestation of the problem," Mrs. King says. "It's all we have to go on."

"I'd just like to see Ellery out of those shades," the nurse says. "Then we can take it from there."

"Would you agree to that?" Mrs. King asks.

"What would happen if he refused to take them off?" I ask.

"He wouldn't be allowed to attend classes. We'd put him in ICE."

"In what?"

"ICE. Isolated Continuing Education. Instead of suspending or expelling our students, we try to keep them in the building, but don't allow them to attend classes or mix with other students."

"It sounds like prison," I say.

"It's a very successful program," Mrs. King says. "It might sound drastic, but it does get us results. Of course it's supplemented with psychological counseling. It's just what some kids need."

"Maybe I should talk to Ellery again," I say.

"By all means, do," says Mrs. King.

"Hey, listen," the nurse says. "We don't want to do anything without your knowledge and cooperation. And it's much better if the problem is approached by you rather than us."

"But there is a problem," says Mrs. King. "And it does have to be approached."

I nod.

"One more question," the nurse says. "I'm just curious. Why did you name him Ellery?"

When I get home from the high school there's a strange car parked in front of the house. I pull into the driveway, and as I walk up the front steps, a woman gets out of the car and crosses the lawn.

"Do you live here?" she asks.

"Yes," I say.

"I came about the garage sale? Vinnie Olloppia—she bought your Osterizer—told me."

"Oh," I say. "Well, come in."

"Where's the stuff?"

"It's inside," I say. "I'm selling the contents of the house."

"Everything?" she asks.

I unlock the front door. "Yes," I say. "We're moving overseas."

"Where to?"

"The Philippines," I say. "My husband is there now. I'm just trying to get the house sold."

"You shouldn't tell people that," the woman says. "I mean, that you're living alone."

"My son is here," I say. And, because Carly is lying in the front hall, I add, "And my dog."

"Does he bite?" the woman asks.

"No," I say.

Carly sighs. We step over him and go into the living room.

"Wow. This is all for sale? Everything?"

"Yes," I say. "My husband's bought a furnished house."

"You could put this in storage," the woman suggests. "I can't imagine selling all my things. Aren't you sad?"

"No," I say. "You can look around. Excuse me a minute."

I go into my bedroom and lie down on the bed. Carly noses open the door and walks over and looks at me. He doesn't like it when you close doors. "Hi, Carly," I say. I stroke his nose, and his ears. Carly has glaucoma and is almost blind. The vet told me that moving him into another new, unfamiliar house would be "torture" for him. Not that we would take him all the way to Manila. We'll have to put him to sleep soon. I'll have to put him to sleep soon.

I can hear the lady walking around the living room. She could be stealing everything, for all I know. That would be nice. That would be the easiest way to get rid of it.

I get up, wash my face, and go back to the living room. The woman isn't there. I go into the kitchen. She's holding open a cupboard door, looking inside. She closes it when she sees me. Real quick.

"I'm sorry," she says.

"No," I say. "It's fine. Look."

"I'm trying to find some things for my daughter. She just got married, and moved into a beautiful condo—in the Riverwarren?—but she won't buy anything for it. She got some things as wedding presents, of course. A bed and a TV and a kitchen table. But she won't get anything else. She doesn't take any interest in fixing the place up. Don't you think that's strange?"

"Yes," I say.

"I'm thinking that if I get a few things, start her off, you know, she'll make an effort. Her husband's just as bad. They lie on the bed, watch TV, and eat frozen food. Oh, she has a microwave, too."

"Would you like something to drink?"

"No, thanks," she says. "Are you selling these pots and pans?"

"Everything," I say.

"How much do you want for these? Are they genuine Revere Ware?"

"Yes," I say. They were my wedding presents. "Twenty dollars?"

"That sounds reasonable." She takes the pots out of the cupboard and arranges them on the kitchen table, stacking them inside of one another. "Listen," she says. "Do you think I could come back with my daughter? Maybe seeing all this stuff, might, you know, excite her."

"Sure," I say.

"But I'll take these pots now. Are you sure just twenty? For the whole set?"

"Yes," I say.

The woman opens her bag and rummages in it. It's shaped like a little wooden picnic basket. She hands me a twenty. "Here you go," she says. "Maybe I'll come back this evening? With Debbie? Would that be O.K.?"

"Sure," I say.

I walk her to the front door. Carly's back in the front hall. We both step over him. He sighs.

I stand inside the door and watch the woman drive away. Then I take the twenty and put it, along with all the other money I've made, in the empty dog biscuit box I keep on top of the refrigerator.

I haven't been sleeping much nights, so I take a nap. Carly joins me. We are awakened by Ellery, home from school, playing his stereo: the soundtrack from *Carousel*. Ellery has strange taste in music.

I knock on his door, and when he doesn't answer I open it. He's lying on his bed, on his back, his sunglasses on. He wears different ones. I forgot to mention that to the guidance counselor. Surely it's not as obsessive if he changes them? The worst are the mirrored ones. The wraparound ones he has on now are thin and curved, so you can't see his eyes, even if you sit beside him and make an effort.

"Hello, Ellery," I say. I turn the music down: "June Is Bustin' Out All Over."

"Hi," Ellery says.

Carly, ignored, noses his chest. "Hello, Carly," Ellery says.

"How was school?" I ask.

"Wonderful," says Ellery. "I learned a lot of new things today."

"I was there," I say.

"I know," says Ellery. "Fiona Fitzhugh told me. She said you had your skirt on backward."

"I didn't have my skirt on backward. It buttons up the back."

"Are you sure?" asks Ellery.

Suddenly, I'm not sure. Have I been wearing it wrong all this time? "You can wear it either way," I rationalize.

"What were you doing in school?" Ellery asks. "Signing up for the bake sale?"

"Is there going to be a bake sale?" I stupidly ask, before I realize he is being sarcastic.

Ellery moans.

"I was seeing Mrs. King. And the nurse. The male nurse."

"I didn't know I was diseased," says Ellery.

"About your sunglasses," I say.

"Ah," says Ellery.

"If you don't stop wearing them, they'll put you on ICE," I say, proud of myself for remembering this vernacular. Maybe it makes up for my bake sale faux pas.

"People say it's actually cooler in ICE. You can put your head down on the desk and sleep if you want."

"Then it would suit you," I say. Ellery smiles, but not being able to see his eyes, it's hard to interpret this smile. I guess it's a mean little smile, though.

"And you're doing irreparable damage to your retinas," I say.

"They can transplant retinas, now, can't they?" Ellery asks.

I think this is a smug remark, especially with poor Carly sitting here with her egg-white eyes. "If you were Carly, you wouldn't say things like that," I say.

Ellery turns away from me, onto his side, so he's facing the wall. He doesn't say anything. From this angle he reminds me of Patrick. Patrick always slept on his side, his bony hip tenting the sheet, forming a little alpine mountainscape. Ellery usually sleeps on his back, the blankets rising smoothly over him, like water.

The record finishes. The needle rises, and clicks itself off. The only sound is Carly's labored breathing. "I'm still here," I say.

Ellery doesn't answer.

"Do you want me to turn the record over?"

He still doesn't answer. And then I notice his back moving:

shaking, ever so slightly, the way it shakes when he's crying, but trying to hold himself still.

I should call Carly and go for a walk, but instead I go into my bedroom and look through Patrick's things. If I had known he was going to die like that, I would have saved everything: his splayed toothbrushes, his outgrown sneakers, every hair that was ever cut from his head. All I have are report cards, pictures, and some Mother's Day cards he made me in Sunday school. When he died, my sister, in a well-intentioned but misguided effort to comfort me, said maybe it was good that Ellery and he were twins, so much alike—that having Ellery was a little like still having Patrick. You have to be their mother to know how absurd that is. There was nothing alike about them. Their elbows were different. Their walks. They had their own auras. For instance, the afternoon I found the bathroom door locked, that awful quiet, I knew it would be Patrick I found inside, once the door was knocked down. I was right. Or: If one of them touched me lightly, with one finger, on my back, I could tell, without turning, without looking, whose finger it was.

I start to make (canned) chili for dinner before I remember I sold all my pots. I keep missing things this way. The other night I went to vacuum and the vacuum was gone. I spoon the opened can of chili into Carly's bowl and call her. She lumbers into the kitchen, smells the food, then sits down, confused, looking at, but not really seeing, me.

"You don't like it?" I say. "It's chili."

Carly just stares. She looks sad. But then dogs always look sad, don't they? That's not true. Carly used to look happy. Sometimes she still grins.

Ellery comes into the kitchen. The hair on one side of his head is bouffanted from sleep. "Is Daddy coming home for dinner?" he asks, although he knows his father is on the other side of our planet.

"He should be home any minute," I say.

"Oh, good," says Ellery. "It will be nice to see him. Are you cooking us a great dinner?"

"You bet," I say, grabbing his shoulders and kissing his neck, before he stops playing whatever game it is we're playing.

Ellery drives us down to Pronto! Pizza!. I'm a little worried about letting him drive with his sunglasses at night, but he appears to see fine, although he's neurotic about signalling: He even puts his blinker on when he turns into the parking space.

Ellery says he doesn't care what kind of pizza we get, and to punish him for his apathy, I order pizza with green peppers, which I know he dislikes. He good-naturedly picks the peppers off his slices, making me feel terrible. I had expected he would complain. Children are always magnanimous when you'd rather they weren't.

"Daddy should call tonight," I say.

"Oh," says Ellery.

If I hadn't ordered the green peppers I would remove them from my slices, too. They taste rubbery and inorganic.

"Will you stay up and talk to him?"

"Maybe," says Ellery. "I'm kind of tired."

"You slept all afternoon."

Ellery shrugs. We eat for a while in silence. Ellery, the fastest eater I've ever known, finishes first and watches me. Or at least I think he's watching (the sunglasses).

"Do you want one of my slices?" I ask. "I can't eat all of this."

"I've made up my mind," Ellery says, ignoring my offer.

"About what?"

"The Philippines," Ellery says.

"What do you mean?" I'm not following him.

"I'm not going."

I put my slice of pizza down, and seeing it, half-eaten on the paper plate, nauseates me. I wipe my greasy hands on a napkin, and cover the remaining pizza with it. "What are you talking about?"

Ellery doesn't say anything. How I wish he would take those sunglasses off.

"What are you talking about?" I repeat, and for the first time, I realize I've been waiting for this: I know.

"I'm not going to move to the Philippines. It just doesn't make sense."

"But I thought you wanted to. We've discussed all this. You're the one who thought it would be so great . . ."

"I've changed my mind," says Ellery. "I still think you should go. I still think it makes sense for you and Daddy."

"And it doesn't make sense for you?"

"No. I have one more year of high school. I'll finish it here, and then get a job. Or go to college, or something."

"And where will you live?"

"Well, at the rate you're selling the house, I can live there. And if you finally sell it, I can live with someone, or something. Or get an apartment."

"And I'm supposed to move to the Philippines and just leave you here?"

"I'm almost eighteen," Ellery says. He begins to stack our refuse on the tray.

"Wait," I say. I take my paper cup of soda and drink from it. Ellery takes the tray and dumps it in the garbage can. He studies the jukebox. I don't know what to do. I feel as if I might start crying, but something about flexing my cheek muscles to sip through the straw comforts me, helps hold my face together. I drain the soda and keep on sucking, inhaling nothing but cold, sweet air.

We drive for a while in silence. Punky-looking kids stand under the streetlights drinking beer.

"Can I drop you off and take the car?" Ellery asks.

"Where are you going?"

"To Fiona Fitzhugh's. We have a physiology lab practical tomorrow and Fiona has the cat."

"What cat?"

"The cat we're dissecting."

"You're dissecting a cat? That's disgusting. Why can't you dissect frogs?"

"One does," Ellery says patiently, "in biology, in ninth grade. In physiology, one dissects cats. Fiona and I are going to quiz each other."

"It sounds romantic," I say.

"It's not a date," Ellery says.

"You're allowed to take the cats home?"

"Not really. But Mr. Gey says that as long as he doesn't see you take it and as long as it's back in the refrigerator by 8:30 he doesn't mind. Fiona has this huge pocketbook. It was easy. Want to hear something?"

"Is it about dissecting cats?"

"No," says Ellery. "People."

"Sure," I say, brightly.

"Mr. Gey was telling us, in the lab where he studies—he's getting his Ph.D. or something—they're dissecting cadavers, and they keep them in this big walk-in freezer and inside the freezer, on the door is a sign that says "YOU ARE NOT LOCKED IN!" Who do you think it's for?

"What do you mean?"

"Do you think it's for the cadavers, you know, if they come back to life, or something, or the people dissecting them, like if they freak out in there?"

"I have no idea," I say. "Who?"

Ellery chuckles. A strange, forgotten sound. "No one knows. Mr. Gey had us vote. With our heads down and everything."

"Does Mr. Gey have a problem?" I ask.

"Mr. Gey is cool," Ellery says.

"Oh," I say. "Well, who did you vote for?"

For a second Ellery doesn't answer. Then he turns to look at me, the streetlights reflecting across his sunglasses. "I voted twice," he says. "I think the sign was there for everyone involved."

Ellery drops me off, and I walk across tufted, crab-grassy lawn, the only imperfect one on our block. There's a note stuck in the front door. It says: "Brought my daughter to see your furniture. Sorry to miss you. We'll come back tomorrow eve. (Wed) If you won't be here will you kindly call?" It's signed Doris Something and underneath that is a phone number. On the other side is a P.S.: "You should leave lights on to discourage burglars."

I'm counting the money in the dog biscuit box when the phone rings. I've counted three hundred dollars, and there's still more. Ellery came home about an hour ago, smelling faintly of formaldehyde, took a shower, and went to bed.

It's tomorrow morning in the Philippines. When I talk to Leonard in these circumstances—he a day ahead of me—I feel as if I've lost him somehow, as if he's lived longer than I; that in the hours he's gained he's learned something I don't know. It's the time, not the distance, that separates us. In the Philippines, Leonard goes home for lunch. He has a chauffeur and a house-keeper. I'm going to love it when I get there. That's what he tells me, when we talk, once a week.

The operator asks for me, and I say I'm me, and then Leonard gets on, and says hello. Sometimes he sounds far away, and sometimes he sounds like he's calling from next door. Tonight he sounds far away. He says he misses me; that he loves me.

Then he asks about Ellery and Carly—I lie and say they're both doing fine—and then he asks about the house. I lie again and tell him someone's about to make an offer.

We talk for a while and then Leonard tells me again how much I will love the house; he bangs the telephone on the floor so I can hear the green slate tiles in the kitchen, and then he starts to hang up.

"Leonard?" I say.

"What?" he says.

"Wait," I say. I'm not sure how I'm going to say what I know I want to say next. We both listen to the static for a moment.

"I don't think I'm going to come," I finally say, listening to my voice unravel across all those miles of cold, dark cable.

"What?" Leonard says.

"Maybe it would better if Ellery and I stayed here."

"What are you talking about?" Leonard asks. "What's happened?"

"Nothing. Nothing's happened. But Ellery doesn't want to move. I think that's good, don't you? I mean, I think he's a little happier here, now. He went on a date tonight."

"Really?" Leonard says. "That's wonderful, great, but that doesn't mean you can't come to the Philippines, Arlene. That's crazy."

"I know," I say. "But . . . maybe you can get transferred back, or something . . ."

"Arlene, I've taken this job. I've got to stay here at least a year, now. At least. I owe them that. And this house . . ."

"I know," I say. "I know that. But it will be O.K. A year . . . I mean, it will only be for a year. That's not too long."

"What are you saying? I don't believe this," Leonard says. "What's happening, Arlene? What about us? I miss you."

"Stop calling me Arlene," I say. Whenever Leonard talks to me on the phone, he keeps inserting my name into the conversation, as if, since he can't see me, he might forget who he's talking to.

"What?" he asks.

"Nothing. I miss you, too," I say. "I do. But . . ."

"But what?"

"I don't think I can move again," I say.

"But Arlene—honey—you're the one who wanted to get the hell away . . . this was your idea."

This is true, but it's not the point. I think for a moment, and then, carefully, say, "No. Not without Ellery."

Leonard doesn't say anything. I listen to our chorus of static.

"Well, this is a real shock," he finally says. "I'm going to have to think about this. Have you thought about this?"

"Yes," I say. "I mean, not really. Ellery just told me."

"Well, why don't we both think about this then? Maybe there's another way to work this. I'll call again tomorrow."

"That sounds good," I say. "I'm sorry."

"Don't be sorry," Leonard says. He pauses. "Is Ellery there? Can I talk to him?"

"He's sleeping," I say. "Do you want me to wake him?"

"Oh, no," says Leonard. "Don't wake him up. Tell him I said . . ."

"What?"

"Tell him I said hi," Leonard says. "Tell him I love him."

After I hang up the phone I let Carly out and stand in the dark backyard with her, watching her squat. I walk down the slope to the clothesline and take down the sheets that have been hanging for a couple of days. They still smell clean, and they feel cool, slightly damp. I think about putting them on my bed: It would be a little like sleeping outdoors. Carly, disoriented, starts to whimper. Her eyesight is especially bad at night. I call her. She walks over to me and inserts her muzzle between my legs: Safe.

We go through the house and I turn all the lights off, burglars or not. I make my bed with the clean, cool sheets, but instead of attempting to sleep, I go into Ellery's room. He doesn't wear his sunglasses in bed. I was very relieved, the first night I came in here, to discover that. It makes it not so bad, somehow. That may sound sick, but you have to measure these things. It's how you bear it. Ellery is lying on his back, his arms akimbo, with one loosely curled fist resting in each eye socket, as if even in sleep there is some bright light he cannot bear.

But it's O.K. I take his hands by their unscathed wrists and gently move them to his side. Ellery doesn't wake up; he assimilates this gesture into the narrative of his dream. His exposed eyelids flicker with secret vision.

WHAT?

Ruth was varnishing the guest room table. She dipped a rag in the pail of amber-colored syrup and stroked the wood, moved it across the top and then down the legs, palming the thin spindles. It's like washing a child, she thought: a child standing up in the bathtub, waiting to sit down and rinse off. She took her time, caressing one leg, then another, letting the varnish soak in. When the fourth leg was done she was disappointed to see the tabletop had lost its wonderful wet gleam. Another coat.

She was on the third, thinking, I can't do this forever, when she heard Joanna arrive with Virgil. Virgil was their dog—well, her dog, now. Joanna had borrowed him for her vacation on Block Island. Two weeks ago Ruth had driven Virgil to the Columbus airport for his flight to Boston. Joanna paid for it all. It was almost as expensive to fly a dog as it was to fly yourself.

Ruth had thought about saying no, forget it, Virgil stays with me, but she hadn't. She knew that Virgil had been waiting for the ocean. Every summer for the six years she and Joanna had been together, Virgil had swum in the surf and chased gulls, and it didn't seem fair to deprive him this late in life. Plus, Ruth had thought, having Virgil there is a little like me being there: There's no way Joanna can help thinking about me, seeing Virgil every day. Or so she hoped.

So Ruth had got tranquilizers from the vet and shipped Virgil east. He arrived so traumatized it took him a couple of days just to walk straight. Joanna couldn't subject him to another flight, so Virgil got driven back to Ohio. That Joanna was kind to animals infuriated Ruth.

The car stopped in front of the house; Ruth heard Virgil bark, and clack up the front steps. Joanna knocked at the front door of the house they had bought together. Jesus, Ruth thought: She knocked.

"Come in," she shouted. "I'm up here." She returned to the table. She hadn't seen Joanna in ten months, and she wanted to be discovered in action.

"Hi," Joanna called, but she didn't come right up. She went into the kitchen and filled a bowl of water for Virgil. Ruth heard Virgil's slurping.

"Virgil," she called. He bounded up the stairs. He was happy to see her. Ruth had to pet him with the inside of her wrists because her hands were sticky with varnish. She rubbed his fur. She kissed him.

Joanna stood in the doorway and watched their reunion. She was drinking a glass of water, taking tiny sips. Ruth remembered: She always does that, gulps one glass fast and then sips the second.

"What are you doing?" Joanna asked, nodding at the table.

"I was trying to varnish this," Ruth said. "But it won't stay shiny."

"It probably needs another coat," said Joanna.

"I've already done three."

"Did you prime it?"

Ruth shook her head no.

"It probably needs to be sealed. And you should be using a brush, not a rag."

Ruth wondered if Joanna knew what she was talking about. She doubted it. "How was the vacation?" she asked.

"Good," Joanna said.

"Were the Goerrings there?"

"Of course," said Joanna, a little tersely, for she hated stupid questions. But she softened. "They asked for you," she said.

"Did you fish?" All Ruth could think of were stupid questions.

Joanna swirled the water in her glass for a second, studying it. "I don't think I want to talk about my vacation," she said.

"Oh," Ruth said.

"Did you make me a reservation at the inn?"

"No," Ruth said.

"What do you mean? I asked you to."

"I called," Ruth lied. "They're full. It's the music festival." It was the music festival: That wasn't a lie. And the inn was always full during the festival. Everyone knew that.

"What about the Travelodge?"

"I'm sure that's full, too. Anyway, don't be absurd. You can stay here. I made up this bed." Ruth pointed to the guest room bed.

"I told you I didn't want to stay here."

"It's just one night," Ruth said. She hid her face in Virgil's neck. He smelled of skunk. She waited for Joanna to say something, but she didn't.

"He got sprayed?" Ruth asked.

"The other night." They looked at each other for a second. Joanna said, "I'll go get my bag."

They ate outside in the dark. Ruth had prepared a meal that was a variation of their usual summer suppers, the same ingredients, but with everything presented just a little differently so the similarity wouldn't be too overt.

"How has your summer been?" Joanna asked.

"Fine," Ruth said.

"How's the book?"

"It's coming." Ruth was writing a book about women's war

fiction. The title was *The Damaged and the Less Damaged*. "How's yours?" she asked.

"I've found a publisher," Joanna said.

"It's finished?" Ruth poured more wine into her glass. In the dark she poured more than she normally would.

"No," Joanna said. "But they saw the chapter in *World Affairs*." Joanna's was a book about hostages through history.

"Who bought it?" Ruth asked.

"Norton."

"That's wonderful," Ruth said. "Congratulations." She could see Joanna smiling. In a way Ruth hated her, but only in a way. It was an intense, flaring hate she couldn't sustain. Mostly she still loved her. Or something like love—love's unidentical, ugly twin: the genes the same, their formation, somehow, askew.

"I'm sure you'll find somebody for yours," Joanna said. "It's just a matter of time."

"Yes," Ruth said.

"So things are going well?"

Ruth shrugged and shook her head. Things were not going well.

"Good," Joanna said, mistaking her gesture. "I'm glad."

They were quiet, listening to the night. The trees were thick with foliage and droning insects, rehearsing for something big. If she were going to say something she should say it now, Ruth thought. This was her chance. She wanted to know when Joanna had stopped loving her. Had she taken the new job in Boston and then stopped, as she claimed, or had she stopped and, consequently, taken the new job? Ruth felt that, if she understood the chronology, all the other questions, the why and the how and the (perhaps) who, all of them would become clear, or cease to matter. What she couldn't stand was looking back, and not knowing when.

"It was very kind of you to drive Virgil home," she said.

"Well, I couldn't have put him back on a plane. It would have been inhuman."

Virgil, who had been sleeping beneath the picnic table, roused himself at the sound of his name.

"I'm going to miss him," Joanna said.

"You could get another dog."

"Not really. Not in an apartment."

"You could get a cat."

"I could." Joanna began examining Virgil's ears for ticks.

"Are you seeing anyone?" Ruth asked.

Joanna looked up at her. "What?" she said.

Ruth repeated her question. In the dark it was easy: You just looked down and away and spoke.

"No," Joanna said.

She's lying, Ruth thought.

"What about you?" Joanna asked.

Ruth shook her head.

"What about Tamar?" Joanna asked.

Tamar was in Slavic Languages. "What about her?"

Joanna had returned her attention to Virgil's ears. "I just thought you might, you know, be interested in Tamar."

"No," Ruth said. "Besides, I don't think she's gay."

Joanna laughed.

"I'm sure she's not," said Ruth. "Besides, it doesn't matter."

"It would if you were interested in her."

"I'm not," Ruth said.

Joanna completed her search by ruffling Virgil's ears. "Finito," she said.

"Did you find any?" Ruth asked.

"No. But he got a lot on the island." Joanna sat back in her chair, and looked about the dark backyard. "How's the garden doing?" she asked.

"Fine," said Ruth. In the dark it looked as if it might be doing fine.

"Could I take some tomatoes back?" Joanna stood up and walked down toward the garden fence.

Ruth followed. "I don't think there are any left," she said. "I've picked all the good ones."

"Have you? Already?"

"Yes," said Ruth. Up close, in the moonlight, the garden looked a mess. She could sense Joanna's not commenting, her wanting to go in and set it all to rights: prune and tie and weed. There is something ruthless about gardening, Ruth thought. It's not natural.

"I canned all the tomatoes," she lied.

"Did you really?" said Joanna.

"Yes. I want to make sauces this winter," Ruth said. "I plan to do a lot of entertaining."

"You'll have to give me a jar," said Joanna.

"Yes," said Ruth. "They're in the pantry." She'll forget, she thought; she forgets everything.

Joanna loitered at the garden's edge.

Ruth said, "You must be tired. All that driving."

"I am," Joanna said. "I think I'll go to bed." She looked up at the stars. She seemed about to say something.

Ruth stood still, waiting.

"Good night," Joanna said.

There were no canned tomatoes in the pantry. There was very little of anything in the pantry, Joanna noticed. She turned out the pantry light and looked around the kitchen. There were several pictures of Devon and Denise, Ruth's nephew and niece, stuck to the refrigerator. Joanna looked at them. They both looked older and less cute. Devon had braces.

Joanna did the dishes she had brought in from outside. Through the kitchen window she could see Ruth sitting at the picnic table, drinking wine and talking to Virgil. It was obvious that she was drunk. This is why I didn't want to stay here, Joanna thought, I didn't want to see this. But she could not look away. It was like one of those violent, fascinating traffic accidents you pass on the highway: debacles you feel compelled, against your better judgment, to observe.

Ruth lay in bed, watching the small, mean hours of the morning go by. At four o'clock she got out of bed. She'd sit in the living room. Maybe Joanna was having trouble sleeping, too. Maybe if she heard her, she'd get up. They could drive out to Dairy Maid for breakfast.

Virgil followed her down the hall. They paused outside the guest room door. Ruth stood for a moment clasping its knob. It was a beautiful knob: cut glass. They had found them in the attic when they bought the house, and restored them.

Ruth opened the door. The moonlight was sudden and bright: It looked as if it had just been turned on. Joanna slept on her stomach, her head mashed into the pillow, her freshly tanned skin dark against the sheets. For a long moment Ruth just stood there, watching.

Joanna raised herself on her arms and turned her head toward them. "What?" she said.

Ruth just stood there.

"What?" Joanna repeated.

Ruth knew she had to say something. "When did you stop?" she asked.

"Stop what?"

"Loving me," Ruth said.

Joanna sunk back into the bed, and then just as quickly threw the sheet aside and swung herself to the floor. Her nakedness was too sudden to be erotic. She began to dress.

"What are you doing?" Ruth asked.

"I'm leaving," Joanna said. "I never should have stayed here."

"Don't leave," Ruth said. "I'm sorry. I just couldn't—I mean, go back to bed. Please, just go back to bed."

Joanna was shoving things in her bag. "I'm leaving," she said.

"It's the middle of the night," Ruth said.

"I'm leaving," Joanna repeated.

"You can't drive now. You're still tired. You'll have an accident."

"I've already had an accident," Joanna said. "This is an accident."

She squeezed by Ruth and ran down the stairs. Ruth and Virgil both followed. The grass was wet. Joanna threw her bag into the car through the open window and then walked around to the driver's side.

Virgil began to bark. Ruth held his collar, which only made him bark louder. He pawed at the side of the car. He wanted to get in. He wanted to go.

"Virgil, no," Ruth yelled. "No, Virgil, no."

Joanna started the car. She had to back down the long driveway, the headlights shining out at Ruth, at her holding Virgil with both hands now, Virgil barking and lunging toward the departing car, their shadows cast behind them onto the scrim of darkness. Joanna turned the headlights off. She backed away without seeing.

After a while Virgil was quiet. It was as if he knew math: Each bark seemed to be interspersed with twice as much silence as its predecessor. When he was done he lay down in the driveway, exhausted from barking and lunging. I wish I were a dog, Ruth thought. I wish I were a dog who could bark bark bark and then be done. She lay down in the driveway beside Virgil. He did not find this odd. He extended his paw and touched her arm.

After a while it was very quiet. Or rather it was no more quiet than it had been but the quietness asserted itself. It came into focus. After a while you couldn't help but be aware of the quiet, no matter what else you were thinking.

If I lie here long enough the sun will rise, Ruth thought. She lay with her ear to the ground, hearing nothing, but thinking of Indians and railroads and buffalo and the car driving away and

Joanna in the car. Above her were stars. They were bright and confused. They were crowding the sky. The more you looked the more you saw. So after a while she stopped looking. She closed her eyes.

Eventually she got up. Virgil got up, too, as if he had been waiting all along. But he hadn't been. He didn't know what was going on. He was, after all, just a dog. It took very little to make him happy. If you petted him and said good dog good dog he was happy. You could make Virgil happy if you wanted to. He followed her inside. There were lights on that Ruth hadn't remembered turning on. She turned them off and stood in the guest room. The unmade bed was something that should be taken outside and burned. And the table: In moonlight, at least, it gleamed.

PART II

~~~~

Someone who excites you
Should be told so, and loved, if you can, but no one
Should be able to shake you so much that you wish to
Give up.

—KENNETH KOCH, *"SOME GENERAL INSTRUCTIONS"*

SLOWLY

Later, this is how we heard it: It was the sixth day of their honeymoon and their last day in Ireland. They decided to drive to the coast, to a beach they had passed the day before, and picnic. At the breakfast table, Jane made a list of what they needed for their meal, and after breakfast Ethan drove the rental car to the closest town and shopped. Jane went for a walk on the bridle path, saw no horses, saw deer, came back to their room, packed their bags, and went down to the terrace and waited. When Ethan had not returned in an hour and a half she mentioned this to the hotel owner, Mr. Fitzgibbon. He told her the stores didn't open till ten; her husband would return by eleven. At noon Mr. Fitzgibbon called the police in Dingle; they told him yes, an American had been in an accident. Driving on the wrong side of the road. Hit by a truck. Deader than—well, dead.

I had been the best man at their wedding. I am—was—Ethan's brother. I had introduced him to Jane Hobard, who had been my friend in college. I stood beside Ethan and watched Jane walk down the aisle. I gave him the ring; I gave it to him, and he gave it to Jane. I watched him slip it down her finger. I woke them at four o'clock the following morning and drove them down the deserted highways to the airport. I helped them unload their bags and then I left them. I kissed Jane good-bye, but I didn't kiss

Ethan. Did I shake his hand? Did I touch his shoulder? I don't remember. Probably not.

Jane did not come to the memorial service. She quit her job and moved to her parents' house on an island in a lake in Canada. I sent her a letter and waited, but got no answer. The summer passed. The week before Labor Day, her brother, Teddy, called me at work in Washington.

"Tom?" he said. "I have a mission that involves you."

"What?" I asked.

"I have been instructed to bring you to Château Hobard this weekend. I am driving up Friday evening and I am not supposed to arrive without you. What are you doing this weekend?"

"Nothing," I said.

"It's Labor Day, you know," said Teddy.

"I know."

"And you don't have plans?"

"No. Well, I was going to Maryland, to my parents'. But . . . Is this Jane's idea?"

"Yes," said Teddy.

"How is she?" I asked.

"I haven't been up in a while. She doesn't talk on the phone. Can you come? If you can get to New York Friday afternoon, I'll drive you the rest of the way."

That night I told Charles about Teddy's mission. "I take it," Charles said, "that I wasn't invited."

"Teddy didn't mention you."

"Château Hobard," Charles said. "Do they really call it that?"

"Yes," I said. "As a joke."

"Well, you should go," said Charles. "You've been summoned." Charles didn't like Jane. I had made the mistake of telling him that if I weren't gay I might have liked to marry Jane myself.

"What will you do?" I asked.

"Nothing," he said. "But don't feel that you're abandoning me."

"You could go out to my parents'," I said.

"You mean spend the weekend with Chester and Ileen? At Château Kildare?"

"Yes," I said.

"You are so wonderfully and pathetically naïve," Charles said.

Château Hobard was reached via a ferry from a small town called Big Bay. Teddy and I arrived there about three o'clock Saturday morning. We had breakfast in a diner and sat in the car, waiting for the first ferry. "Last summer I did this with Ethan," Teddy said. "It was Labor Day, too."

"I remember," I said. "It was when they got engaged."

"It's a shame," said Teddy.

I didn't say anything.

"I taught him how to wind-surf that weekend. He was terrible."

"He wasn't an athlete," I said. "I got all the athletic genes."

"That's funny," said Teddy. After a while he fell asleep; at least he slumped forward and drooled. I liked Teddy. I reclined his seat and pushed him back into it; he woke for a second and smiled at me, wiped the spittle from his face, and fell back asleep. I got out of the car and walked through the deserted town, looking in the shop windows at the mannequins and lawn mowers and books. In the half-darkness they all looked vaguely alike. Everything seemed just on the verge of being alive, poised on the edge of gesticulation. I thought about running away, finding the bus or train or taxi station and disappearing north into the wilderness. But I went nowhere. As it got light I could see the island across the lake, and as the sun rose it struck the fronts of houses there. Windows gleamed as if they had lanterns hung in them. As if the houses were on fire.

"Jane has gone to pick berries," Mrs. Hobard said. "She claims she will bake a pie."

"Oh," I said. And then, "What kind of berries?" I couldn't think of what else to say. Mrs. Hobard was showing me my room. The house was old and made of stone; my room was in a kind of tower.

"Gooseberries," said Mrs. Hobard. "There is a thicket of them up past the barn. Did you notice the barn?"

"No," I said.

"It's straight down the driveway and across the field. If you follow the path behind it—the dirt path, not the gravel one— you'll find the berries. And, I hope, Jane. Why don't you go help her?"

"O.K.," I said.

"There's an extra blanket in here," said Mrs. Hobard, opening an armoire. "It gets cold at night." She laid the blanket across the foot of the bed.

"How is Jane?" I asked.

Mrs. Hobard smoothed the blanket. "I don't know," she said. "She doesn't talk about it. I think it's good she wants to see you." She looked up at me. "Go find her," she said. "Tell her to come home for lunch."

I followed the dirt path up through the woods to a small meadow. It was the highest point on the island. I could see the lake on all sides, filled now with boats and event, although it was quiet up on the bluff. The gooseberry bushes ringed the field. They were low and scrubby and full of tent caterpillars, not berries. I walked across the meadow and found Jane lying asleep in the hot tall grass. I stood and watched her. She was lying on her back, her arms crossed over her breasts, her face turned to one side. I knelt down and looked in her pail. There were some berries in it, but mostly it was full of other things: twigs and stones and flowers. A toad leapt up against the curved cool metal, falling back into the debris. I set him free.

*   *   *

"Jane," I said, and my voice sounded awful, the way I've heard it when it has been recorded and played back. I moved my hand above her face so it blocked the sun, shadowed her eyes.

They opened. She smiled at me for a moment and then sat up. "Hello," she said.

"Hi," I said.

"I was sleeping," she said. "What time is it?"

"About noon." I looked up at the sun, as if I could tell time by it. It did seem to be at the top of the sky. "Your mother says to come home for lunch."

"You came," she said.

"Yes. With Teddy."

"You've never been here," she said. "What do you think?"

"It's beautiful," I said.

"You saw the house?"

"Yes."

"I got your letter," she said. "Thanks."

I shrugged. I sat down. She picked up her bucket.

"I let the frog go," I said.

"It was a toad."

"I let him go," I repeated. "He went thataway."

"I think I'm still a little asleep," said Jane. She looked up at the sky. "I sleep all the time now," she said. "I was taking these tranquilizers, but I'm not anymore. But I still sleep."

"Sleeping's cool," I said.

"I was hysterical for a while," said Jane. "You missed it. Now I'm not hysterical anymore. I just sleep."

"Should we pick more berries?" I asked.

She looked in the bucket. "The toad probably peed on all of these," she said. She emptied the bucket onto the place where she had been sleeping: the warm, matted grass. "Let's go have some lunch," she said.

"O.K.," I said. I started walking toward the path.

"Wait," said Jane. "Come here. We have to hug. I want to hug you."

I stepped through the grass and hugged her. I knew she was crying by the way she shook, and then I heard it. I held her and looked out at the water. Then I looked down at the berries and petals strewn in the grass. I closed my eyes.

"Sometimes I can't stop," Jane said, as we walked down the path through the trees. "The first time I went to Big Bay—the only time, actually—I got completely hysterical. It was rather wonderful. I went over to see *Born Free*—you know, about the lions. They show a movie at the high school every Saturday night. Very rinky-dink. Anyway, it was a big deal: my first trip to the mainland. Back to life, I guess. I went with my parents. We had dinner at the hotel, and I was fine. I was quite ordinary. I had dessert and everything. And then we went to the movie, which was in the gym—all these folding chairs and a movie screen under the basketball hoop. You would have loved it. About two minutes into it, the man-eating lion kills the native woman washing her clothes. You don't even know the woman, you've developed no sympathy for her. I mean, she's not a character. She's just this woman. Well, I completely lost it. I started crying, and I couldn't stop. All the way back home on the ferry, I cried, and when we got home they wanted to take me back over to the doctor, and somehow that stopped me. The idea of distance. Of traveling. I realized I just wanted to go to bed. You get to a point where you don't want to cry anymore, at least not cry and travel, and then it's easy to stop. That's when I started taking the tranquilizers."

"But you've stopped?"

"Yes. I don't need them anymore. I'm fine."

I looked at her. We had emerged from the woods into the pasture behind the barn. "You're fine?" I asked.

"I mean I'm better," she said. "How are you?"

There was a tree in the field and some cows lying underneath it. They seemed to be watching us. "I'm better, too," I said.

We stood for a moment, watching the cows. Jane mooed. It sounded authentic to me, but the cows took no notice.

That night, after dinner, we sat on the terrace and watched the sun set. Barrels of salmon-colored geraniums separated the flagstones from the lawn, which sloped down the hill to the lake, where it ended abruptly, as if it were a scene in a child's coloring book: lawn, water; green, blue. At the same moment in the evening's descent, when the light from the sun was falling most beautifully through the clouds, groundhogs appeared from the earth and sat, Buddha-like, on the lawn. They seemed to be waiting to sing: something ancient, in unison.

We were all there: the parents Hobard, Teddy, Jane's younger sister Eleanor, her boyfriend Scott, Jane, and I. No one said anything. We watched the sun and the groundhogs as if they were fascinating and specially rehearsed.

"There's an albino one," Eleanor finally said. "Scott and I saw it the other night. He looks like a baby polar bear."

"I've never heard of an albino groundhog," said Mrs. Hobard.

"There are albino everything," said Eleanor.

"I bet it was a rabbit," said Mrs. Hobard.

"It wasn't a rabbit," said Eleanor. "What would a rabbit be doing in a groundhog burrow?"

"Vacationing?" suggested Mrs. Hobard.

The sun and the groundhogs departed simultaneously. Mr. Hobard lit kerosene torches, and we watched bats swoop from one side of the lawn to the other. Crickets chirped. We played a game called adverbs, which was a little like charades. People had to act out a scene in the manner of an adverb while someone tried to guess what the adverb was. Mr. Hobard was dismissed to be the guesser. We decided on "surreptitiously." Mr. Hobard returned, and directed Mrs. Hobard to sell Eleanor a hat in the manner of the word. Mr. Hobard guessed "incompetently" and "lackadaisically." New participants and a new scenario were needed. While Scott tried to surreptitiously teach Teddy German, I looked across the firelit terrace at Jane, who was sitting on a wrought iron bench, looking down at the lake. Her cheeks and eyes were wet. I knew why she was crying, or at least I thought I did: It should have been Ethan sitting here, across the patio, or, better yet, beside her on the bench; it should have been Ethan she had canoed with that afternoon; it should have been Ethan—my brother Ethan—who woke her in the field surrounded by gooseberry bushes. That is why I thought she was crying; that is why I cried.

I got up and moved down the lawn, out of the hot flickering light, into the shadowed, bumpy groundhog turf. Behind me, the adverb was declared too difficult and the game abandoned. "You must be exhausted, Thomas," Mrs. Hobard called out to me, "and you, too, Teddy, driving all last night. I think we're all tired."

"I'm not," said Eleanor. "I'm going to swim. Do you want to swim, Scott?"

"No," said Scott, "Swimming in the dark water gives me the creeps."

"It's beautiful at night," said Eleanor. "Will you come, Jane?"

Jane stood up. "I'll come watch you," she said. "You shouldn't swim alone."

"Let's take the canoe out," said Eleanor. "We'll look in the swamp for fox fire." The two of them set off down the lawn.

"Be careful," called Mrs. Hobard.

We watched their shapes disappear toward the lake, into the trees, and then heard the canoe being launched, the slow splash of paddles, their voices. Then it was quiet.

I said good night and went up to my room in the tower. I couldn't find the light switch so I undressed in the dark. I opened the windows and leaned out into the night. The torches had been extinguished. I could hear the click of billiard balls from downstairs and, in the far distance, Eleanor's laugh. A splash.

In bed I thought about Ethan, just missing him. I realized I did not want to be there anymore, in that tower room of Château Hobard. It was not that I thought it was haunted. It was that I wished it were.

"My turn to wake you up," Jane said. She was standing beside my bed, grinning down at me. It was still dark. "I've been watching you sleep," she said. "You sleep the untroubled sleep of angels."

"How long have you been watching?" I asked.

"Not long. What were you dreaming about?"

"I don't know. I don't think I was dreaming."

"Of course you were. I could tell. Were you dreaming of Charles?"

"No," I said.

Jane sat down on the window seat beside the bed and kicked off her shoes. "How is Charles? I forgot to tell you how pleased I was to meet him. It was nice of you to bring him to the wedding."

"He said to say hello," I lied.

"He's awfully good-looking," said Jane, "and he can dance. Did you know that? Do you ever dance together?"

"No," I said.

"That's sad," said Jane. "You should." She opened the window. "Eleanor's still out in the canoe. She got Scott to go with her. They went over to the hotel for a drink."

"What have you been doing?" I asked.

"Waiting. I won't be able to sleep until they get back." She looked out at the lake. "I think I saw the northern lights before. I was walking around the lake. I mean around the island. Come here. Come watch the sky."

"I can see from here," I said.

"But not properly," she said.

"It's too cold. I haven't got anything on."

"You're such a prude." She stood up and sat down beside me on the bed. "Move over," she said. "I'm coming in."

"There isn't much room," I said.

She got in bed beside me. For a while we said nothing. "Don't fall asleep," she said.

"I'm not," I said.

"So are you in love with this Charles?"

"I don't know," I said.

"Of course you do," she said.

"He's going to Africa," I said.

"To be an ambassador?"

"Economic attaché, at an embassy."

"Are you going with him?"

"I don't know. I doubt it."

"Why?"

"I don't think he wants me to come. I don't think the State Department does, either."

"Have you asked him?"

"Not really," I said.

"Maybe we should go to Africa, the two of us. We'll move to Africa and start a coffee plantation. At the foot of the Ngong Hills."

"Perfect," I said.

"Good," she said, "So it's all settled."

"Perfect," I repeated, sleepily.

"Don't fall asleep," Jane said.

"I won't."

We heard Eleanor's laugh out on the lake. Jane sat up. "They're coming home," she said. "In the wake of the moon. It looks lovely." She watched Eleanor and Scott paddle toward the shore. "I think they want to get married," she said.

"So why don't they?" I asked.

"Because of me. They're waiting on my account. For me to get over this."

"That's very sweet," I said.

"I know," said Jane. "Everyone's sweet. I hate it."

"Do you think I'm being sweet?"

"You're being sweetish," said Jane.

"I'm sorry."

"That was sweet," said Jane.

I didn't say anything. We lay in bed, listening to Eleanor and Scott come into the house. We listened to them climb the stairs, use the bathroom, get into bed. We listened to them make love. Then everything was quiet for a long time.

"Are you asleep?" I finally asked.

"No," said Jane. "Do you want me to leave?"

"No," I said.

"It's all right if I sleep here?"

"If you want," I said.

She turned and put her face against my neck. "You smell like him," she said. I didn't say anything. She must have felt me tense up because she laid a hand on my chest, over my heart, and said "Relax."

I tried to relax. I looked up at the ceiling. Jane continued to speak into my throat. "Did you get a postcard from Ethan?" she asked.

"Yes," I said.

"He mailed them that morning. We had written them the night before, on the terrace. We were staying at a castle. It wasn't really a castle, but they called it one. A cheat." She paused. She lifted her face away from my throat, and I could tell she was looking down at me. I continued to look at the ceiling.

"I think he knew what was going to happen," she said. "I mean, in some way he knew. Some instinctual way. He sent me a postcard. He bought it in town that morning. It was of the church in Dingle." She stopped talking. I thought she might cry.

"And what did it say?" I asked. I looked at her.

She wasn't crying. Her face was bright, her eyes and skin shone. "It said, 'Having a wonderful time. You are here.'"

*　　*　　*

Teddy was staying the week at the lake, so I went home alone. I took a bus to Toronto and flew to Washington. I got home about nine o'clock at night. Charles was out at some embassy reception. I got in bed and waited for him. I fell asleep and awoke an hour later to see Charles standing in the semi-darkness, removing his tuxedo. I felt a little as if I were dreaming. I lay there and watched him. He watched me. He unknotted his tie and it slithered out from his collar. He unwrapped his cummerbund. He unstudded his studs.

"I want to come to Africa," I said, once he was in bed.

"So come to Africa," he said.

"Do you want me to come to Africa?" I asked.

"Of course," he said. "What would Africa be without you?"

I thought for a moment. "Hot," I said. "And beautiful. Full of baobab trees, and lions."

"Exactly," said Charles.

for Stephanie Gunn

THE MEETING
AND GREETING AREA

The new "Education" Government, in its quest for literacy, has labeled everything. The buses proclaim BUS, the benches BENCH. I was awaiting the arrival of my ex-boyfriend, Tom, in THE MEETING AND GREETING AREA of the AIRPORT.

I hadn't seen Tom in six months, since I was posted here. Before that we had lived together in Washington, D.C. We broke up shortly before I moved. We fell slowly out of love, paratroopers, floating back down to earth, landing with a quiet thud: friends. So when Tom called and asked me if I would like a visitor, if I would travel with him as we had once planned, I said yes.

"Are you sure?" he asked, his familiar voice echoing itself.

"Of course," I said. "It will be fun. You're my favorite person to travel with. We can go up north to the mountains, where it will be cool."

"Wherever," said Tom. "It's up to you. I just want to get out of D.C. And I'd like to see you. How are you doing?"

I debated telling him about Albert, but I didn't, because Albert was something I hadn't yet figured out. "I'm fine," I said, and I heard my echo say *I'm fine,* as if I had repeated myself for emphasis.

*   *   *

THE MEETING AND GREETING AREA was empty. Dust blew in from the runway and was roiled by the overhead fans, each of which revolved at its own particular speed. Tom's plane was intimated rather than announced. A murmuring excitement spread through the building: Vendors woke from their drowse and dusted their ancient merchandise; the baggage wheel shuddered and began to rotate; the lights above the ticket counter flickered on. And then the plane itself appeared in a huge sky pulsing with heat.

For such a big thing it disgorged few passengers. They appeared at the top of the metal steps hastily appended to its side, one by one, like bewildered contestants, blinking at the bright sun, stunned by the heat. Tom, as polite as he is patient, was the last to emerge. I watched him glance out and around, looking for me, and I enjoyed that moment of seeing him before he saw me. It made me feel in control. I didn't move or call out—I stood still and let Tom find me.

"It's great," Tom said. "And wow, you even have a terrace."

"Everyone has a terrace here," I said. "Most people live on them. Only foreigners have air conditioning."

"Is it always this hot?"

"You get used to it," I said.

He was standing by the French doors, looking down into the garden. A woman was washing clothes in the fountain. He looked at me. "I'm excited," he said. "I'm happy to be here." He came over and touched me. We had embraced once, briefly, outside the airport. Tom had smelled of toothpaste and cologne; I could picture him performing a brief ablution in the tiny bathroom of the plane as it bumped in over the mountains.

"Are you exhausted?" I asked. "Or hungry? I thought we could go get some lunch. There's a café at the bazaar."

"It might be nice to lie down," he said. "Just for a little while.

I'm not really that hungry. I still can't believe I'm here."

"You are," I said.

We looked at each other, and then Tom looked away. "I've missed you," he said. "Seeing you makes me realize. It's weird."

This admission seemed to embarrass both of us. "I brought all the things you asked for," Tom continued. "Here, I'll show you." He opened his suitcase and removed a plastic bag of groceries: peanut butter, salad dressing, jam, a squat ball of Gouda. An elegant bottle of vodka.

"Thank you," I said. "Should we have a drink to celebrate your arrival?" A drink suddenly seemed a good idea.

"Sure," Tom said. "Whatever."

The telephone rang. "Hello," I said.

"Mission accomplished?" asked Albert.

"We just got back."

"Is it awful?"

"No," I said.

"Charles, darling, tell me."

"It's fine," I said.

"He's listening, isn't he?"

"Of course," I said.

"So it is awful," said Albert.

"It's not," I said. "We're going out to lunch. I'll talk to you later."

"I hope you'll do more than talk," said Albert.

"Good-bye," I said. "Thanks for calling."

"Wait," said Albert.

"What?"

"Don't forget tomorrow night, will you?"

"No. What time do you want us?"

"Probably eight. I'll have Irene give you a call, how would that be? Wouldn't that be proper? To have the hostess call you? You know how I like to do things properly."

"I know," I said.

"I miss you already," said Albert. "Do you miss me?"

"It goes without saying," I said, and hung up.

We brought the elegant bottle of vodka to the café. As the place emptied, we loitered at our table. The combination of my drunkenness and Tom's jet lag suited us to each other, and we spent a few hot hours in an easy camaraderie I was afraid we might have lost. A beautiful somnambulistic boy mated pairs of chairs on top of tables, overturning one onto the lap of the other. Then he swabbed the floor with a mop and a pail of dirty water. We watched him as if he were the main attraction of a floor show.

"We could go walk around the old town," I finally suggested.

"O.K.," Tom said. "In a while. It's nice just to sit here."

"Is it how you pictured?"

"I don't think so." He looked around. "But I always forget how I pictured something once I actually see it. I mean, I know I had this picture in my mind, but now it's gone."

"I know that feeling," I said.

The boy with the mop paused and leaned against it, resting. It looked as if he had fallen asleep, standing up, holding the mop.

"What goes without saying?" asked Tom.

"What?"

"Before, on the phone. You said something went without saying. What?"

"I forget," I said. "Something about work."

"That was someone from work?"

"In a way. He's with the French Embassy. We're going to his house for dinner tomorrow night."

"How did you meet him?"

"At a party."

"I thought you hated parties."

The boy tottered, awoke, and continued his job. "I do," I said. "But there isn't much else to do over here. Besides, it's important to meet people, starting out."

"Of course," said Tom. He paused. "Is he gay?"

For a moment I thought he meant the boy. Then I realized he meant Albert. "Oh, no," I said. "He's married. You'll meet his wife tomorrow."

For a brief moment, when I first met Albert at a reception in the turquoise-walled garden of the French Consulate, I thought he was ugly, his beauty is so distinct. He has a strangely elongated onslaught of a face, rather like that of a Bedlington terrier. It is the sort of preternatural face that implies there are idiots in the family, that the genes that had found amazement here must surely have collided less fortunately elsewhere.

Albert was married to a large, beautiful woman named Irene. She was not very bright, but she dressed well and could muster herself to the dim verge of charm. She drank, and handwrote all the invitations to embassy events in her beautiful conventual script. Her bedroom was separate from Albert's. They had what he called an "English" marriage.

The sun had gone down somewhere but from where we sat in the garden of the French Consulate it looked as if the sun had gone down behind everything. The air was just beginning to cool or, more aptly, become less hot. A large pitcher of martinis sweated on a carved teak table.

"So you come to us from New York?" Irene asked Thomas.

"Washington," said Tom.

"Ah, yes, Washington. I loathe Washington. Albert and I spent a dreadful year there. When was it darling? Eighty-three?"

"Eighty-two," said Albert.

"That's right," said Irene. "I found them surprisingly backward in Washington. Of course everything is relative. The situation here is hopeless."

"It seems very beautiful here," said Tom.

Irene looked around the garden. "Oh," she said, "but beauty is only half the game, and the easy half at that. A city needs more than beauty. It needs charm, and it needs energy. Of course I am partial, but I believe Paris to be a perfect city. Would you agree?"

"I have never been to Paris," says Tom.

"Have you really not? Imagine coming all this way, to this god-forsaken spot, and never seeing Paris. It is criminal. But then I envy you, because you have that to look forward to: entering Paris for the first time."

"How does one enter Paris?" Tom asked.

Irene looked up into the sky. It was the same purple color as her dress, but it was inexorably darkening and her dress was not. "Oh," she said. "I was wrong to mention Paris. It only makes me sad."

"Irene grew up in Paris," said Albert. "She has never forgiven me for taking her away."

Irene smiled and reached out to pat Albert's cheek. "That is the least of what I haven't forgiven you for," she said.

After dinner, while Irene showed Tom her collection of gold snuffboxes, Albert and I smoked on the veranda. Tall gecko-filled trees rose up from the dense, imported foliage below. The lizards inhabited the trees as disinterestedly as lichen.

"He's so . . . enthusiastic," said Albert. "And simple."

I smiled. I had drunk more than I ought. The veranda seemed to be pitching in some silent nonexistent breeze. I held onto its marble balustrade and closed my eyes. "Actually, he's very smart," I said.

"Oh, I'm sure he is. In a simple, enthusiastic sort of way."

"You shouldn't say mean things about him," I said.

Albert inhaled. His cigar lit up, and for a second I could see all the furiously focused sparks of it. Then they went out. "May I tell you something?" he asked.

"What?" I said.

"Thomas still loves you," Albert said.

"What makes you say that?"

"Because I can tell he is in love. And I doubt seriously it is with either me or Irene. That leaves you, Charles."

"How can you tell he's in love?" I asked.

"You forget I've had some experience with these things." Albert traced the route of a blue vein up my forearm with a manicured finger.

I pulled my arm away. "Tom's my friend," I said. "I'm very fond of him, but he's just my friend."

"Famous last words," said Albert.

"I don't want to talk about this," I said.

"Of course you don't," Albert said. "This is precisely the sort of thing you avoid talking about."

"It's not my fault if Tom loves me," I said.

"I didn't say it was."

"I don't love Tom," I said. "I love you." I said this partially to disarm Albert and partially to see if it might be true. I couldn't tell. I was about to repeat it when the shutters opened. Irene and Tom appeared, silhouetted against the brilliantly lit drawing room. For a moment everyone stood still.

"When do you boys head north?" Albert asked.

"Tomorrow," I said.

"You're going up to Kunda?" Irene asked.

"Yes," I said. "And Lake Moore. And then we're going down south."

"You'd better be careful. There's been some trouble up north," Albert said. "I hear the border is hot."

"What did you think of them?" I asked. Tom and I were walking home along the muddy unmotivated river that curled through the city. I had yet to figure out in which direction it was supposed to flow, never having seen it do so.

"Irene seemed a little crazy."

"She was drunk."

"I know, but she seemed crazy, too. She tried to give me one of those snuffboxes."

"You should have taken it," I said. "What did you talk about up there?"

Tom smiled. He was kicking a piece of glass along the cobblestoned street, paying it concentrated, irksome attention. I intervened and kicked it into the river, which swallowed it without a ripple.

"I forget," Tom said.

"What did you think of Albert?"

Tom looked at me. "He's charming," he said. "In a neo-fascist kind of way."

"What do you mean?"

Tom was scuffing the pavement, looking for something else to kick. He seemed nervous. A posse of nuns on bicycles passed us, and then disappeared. The city was full of nuns. I decided to change the subject.

"So," I said. "Tomorrow we head north. Let's hope it will be cooler."

Tom stopped walking, and leaned against the river wall. A dugout canoe with a goat tethered in it was moored in the middle of the river. The goat bleated at us.

"I don't think I'm going," said Tom.

"What?" I said.

"I think maybe I should go home."

"What do you mean? You just got here."

"I know that," said Tom.

"So why do you want to go back?"

"I have a feeling maybe this won't work out."

"Why wouldn't it work out?"

Tom looked at me. He shrugged. "It's just a feeling," he said.

"It will be fine," I said. "We'll spend some time in Kunda, it will be cool and beautiful. Kunda's supposed to be really great. We like to travel together. We're good at it. Why would there be a problem?"

Tom stared at the river, at the goat in the boat, and on the far shore at the abandoned skeletons of the office buildings the Commerce Government had begun to build before its recent demise. I put my hand on his shoulder. "Everything's cool, Tommy," I said. "Relax."

I was sitting up in the king-size bed in our hotel room, safe within a flurry of mosquito netting. Tom stood beside the bed, wearing a pair of gym shorts, drying his hair with a towel monogrammed "The Royal Kunda."

"There's a lizard in the bathroom," said Tom.

"Better lizards than bugs," I said.

"There are bugs, too," said Tom. "Are you going to take a shower?"

"I'll take one in the morning."

"I've never slept under a mosquito net," Tom said. Tom is the sort of person who takes delight in doing things for the first time. He is constantly losing some sort of virginity. I once found this quality endearing. He touched the gauze shroud. "How do you get in? Do you climb under?"

"You lift it up," I said.

"Oh." He returned the towel to the bathroom, bolted the door, switched off the light, and resumed his post beside the bed. The combination of the gauze and dark masked his features, but I could feel him looking at me.

"Get in," I said. "Let's go to sleep."

He lifted the net and stooped beneath it, and then he was inside, better focused, large and luminous. I thought of him entering Paris for the first time. I moved to one side of the bed as he got in. We lay side by side for a long, silent while. I could smell his clean skin. And then, like a perfectly scheduled train, I saw his hand set out across the blank expanse of sheet between us. For a moment I thought my anticipation and dread had set it in motion—that I had somehow willed him to touch me by dreading he might. And then he did touch me; his fingers slid up and gently clasped my arm right below my elbow. It was an odd, unerotic place to hold someone. It was where you'd hold someone to pull him back from traffic, or other sudden dangers.

Kunda was full of Germans, cafés, elephants, and posters of blond women fellating bottles of Coca-Cola. Most of the buildings were made of mud; it was hard to believe that come the rains, they wouldn't all wash away.

We had wandered down through town all morning, from one terraced level to another, and noon found us on its grassy outskirts.

"We could visit the fish caves," said Tom, who was in possession of our tourist map.

"What are the fish caves?"

"I don't know. It's just on the map with a blue star. That means it's a natural phenomenon."

"Where are they?"

"Just a little bit out of town, going east." He pointed down the road.

"How far?"

"You look. I say about a mile."

We started walking east out of town. Along the roadside, people were sitting beneath jerry-built tents, trying to sell the odd objects spread out before them: gourds, widowed shoes, and strange cuts of meat swaddled in leaves. One woman had dozens of cheeping sparrows in tiny cages woven from sticks. The cages were only barely bigger than the birds. Her sign read: PLEASE SET FREE THESE BIRDS YOU WILL BE HAPPY AND PROSPEROUS. We passed the woman and turned off the road at a sign that said FAMOUS FISH CAVES. Inside a spectacular wrought iron gate a beautiful woman was selling little bunches of what appeared to be salad. Each bunch was wrapped in colored wax paper. She held them in a tray projecting from her chest, like a New Age cigarette girl.

"You buy some," she told us.

We declined her offer and walked down the path into the dry, scrubby woods. She followed us at a distance. We approached an enclave of massive boulders which surrounded a small pool of dark still water.

The woman had caught up with us. "Fish cave," she announced.

We all stood and stared at the water. The air around us was surprisingly cool. "Where are the fish?" I finally asked.

The woman indicated her colorful packages. "For food, they'll come," she said.

"That's fish food?" asked Tom.

"Yes," she said.

"It's so pretty," said Tom.

"They are special fish," she said. "You'll see if you feed them."

"How much?"

She told him, and he bought a package of greens. The care with which it had been assembled necessitated his unfolding it with reverence. Tom held a little bouquet of strange-shaped leaves and yellow clover-like flowers.

"Feed them." The beautiful woman was losing patience. She glanced back toward the gate, but we were still alone.

"All at once?" Tom asked.

She shrugged.

Tom tossed the bouquet into the black water. It spun idly for a moment, and then the pool erupted with huge blue carp. They churned the water into froth, leaping at the weeds. When they had devoured Tom's bouquet they loitered near the surface, swishing their tails, watching us.

"More?" the beautiful woman asked.

The ritual was repeated: the tossing, the feeding frenzy, followed by the blue-tinted, tail-flashing shallow lurk.

"More?"

I had the feeling we could be there forever, that those horrible fat fish would never be sated. "Let's go," I said.

"O.K.," said Tom. "No, thank you," he said to the woman. She turned and walked back toward the gate.

Tom and I remained at the fish cave. The fish sank lower as time passed, like something being erased, until the water returned to its primordial blankness. "That was something," Tom finally said. "I've never seen fish like that."

"They were more like pigs," I said.

Tom squatted and dipped his hand into the water. "It's freezing," he announced. We both watched his hand float, palm up, just below the water's dark skin. It made me nervous: The fishes' appetite had seemed carnivorous. I had a feeling Tom not only sensed but enjoyed my unease, so I squatted beside him and dangled my fingers in the water. His hand swam toward mine. Our fingers touched, but the water was so cold I couldn't feel it. I let my hand drift away.

"It's much cooler here than back in town," Tom said. "It would be a nice place for a picnic."

"We don't have anything to eat," I said.

"Let's just sit down for a while," said Tom. "Over there, by those trees."

I followed him to a grassy clearing in the flowering trees where the sun was haphazardly strewn across the ground. Bees buzzed around us.

"This is beautiful," said Tom. He was lying on his back, his head pillowed by his knapsack, his eyes closed. I stood against the tree and watched him. His hands were clasped behind his head, his face angled toward the sun. Tom loved the sun. I first saw him three years ago, on the beach at Edisto. It was very early in the morning, and the beach was empty. Tom had been lying alone in much the same position as he lay now. For a moment I thought he was dead but then I realized he was sleeping. I stood and watched him. Normally I would never stop and watch someone sleep on the beach but I was not acting normally when I met Tom, and that is how you fall in love: by not being yourself or being too much yourself or by letting go of yourself, and I did one, or perhaps all, of those things; I stood and waited for Tom to wake up and he woke up and I sat down beside him on the cool sand. And now, as I watched Tom lie in the sun here on the other side of the earth years later, I wondered if perhaps I did still love him. But what I felt was an awful staining fondness, not love.

The beautiful woman was escorting two German couples toward the fish cave. Tom opened his eyes. We watched them disappear behind the rocks. "So," said Tom. "Here we are."

"Yes," I said.

"Sit down," said Tom.

I sat down, a little wary: Tom always initiated a troubling conversation by saying "So." Whenever he said *so*, I heard *beware.*

"It's nice to lie here in the sun," he said, "and think of everyone shivering back home. It gives me great pleasure."

"Good," I said, and I meant it, as I was glad Tom was experiencing great pleasure. This was not something he often admitted.

"Actually," said Tom, "I'm not feeling great pleasure."

"Oh," I said.

"Actually, I'm feeling kind of desperate."

"About what?" I asked.

"About this," said Tom. "About us."

I said Oh again. Tom looked at me. "What are you feeling?" he asked.

There is only one question I hate more than "What are you feeling?" and that is "What are you thinking?" I believe one should be at liberty to express one's thoughts and feelings at one's own pace; to be prompted in this way is, I think, rude. I know for a fact Tom thinks otherwise. He thinks he is doing me a favor by asking these questions, but it is dangerous and stupid of him, for the responses he elicits are seldom the responses he desires. In answer to his question, I said, "What am I feeling about what?"

"Us," he said.

I shrugged. I heard the Germans exclaim over the appearance of the blue fish. I pretended to be distracted by their exclamations. "I don't know," I finally said. "I'm not feeling anything. I'm just glad, you know, that we're together, that we're friends, that we're traveling together. I think it's nice."

"Nice?" said Tom.

"I think it is," I said. "Don't you?"

Tom didn't answer. He closed his eyes. His face was no longer in the sunlight; it was laced with shade. "It's not obvious?" he asked.

"What?" I said, although of course I knew. I had known from the very beginning, from the moment Tom had crossed the tarmac and entered THE MEETING AND GREETING AREA. I had not needed Albert to tell me.

"I still love you," he said. He opened his eyes.

I didn't know what to say so I said nothing. How pathetic the unloved are, I thought. How assiduously they suffer, how they cultivate their rejection, picking again and again at their scabs.

"I just thought I should tell you," said Tom. "Although I guess I shouldn't have."

"No," I said. "I mean, I just thought, you know, that that was all over."

"I know," said Tom. "So did I."

"It's over for me," I said.

"I know," said Tom. "I know that." He stood up, and hoisted his knapsack to his shoulder. "Forget I said anything," he said. "Let's go." He began to walk back toward the road. I followed him. On the way into town we stopped and liberated a bird. Tom tore the twig cage apart. The bird jumped out and sat by the side of the dusty road. I tried to make it fly by prodding it with a stick but it wouldn't. It just sat there, stunned, it seemed, by its freedom.

Albert was right: The border was hot. That morning insurgents had invaded a mountain village. We returned to find Kunda tense with outrage and excitement and plans for a nationalist rally in the public garden that evening.

Tom and I observed from the refreshment tent, which was packed with curious, intoxicated tourists, including the two German couples from the fish cave. A marching band ringed the arid fountain, and on the grassy verges between the tree-lined paths different groups assembled. Schoolchildren, scrubbed and dressed in their blue uniforms, convened at one end of the park. They held placards—OUR BORDERS ARE SACRED—above their heads, while at the other end of the park the women milled, dressed in traditional costume, a little embarrassed by the hoopla, watching the more fervent, fist-waving men try to organize themselves into some sort of parade.

And as we watched, a parade evolved: The band led the children out of the park, followed by the women, and finally the men. It circled the large square, but since it appeared that everyone in town was marching, the parade's effect was curiously hollow. We tourists, by the very fact of our foreignness, could not even succeed as spectators. We observed in polite silence. After one revolution the marchers halted; the men hushed the band and murmured among themselves. The women and children stood about, abject and quiet. And then the men emerged from their huddle and announced their solution, which, as they reconvened, became obvious: This time the men would march and the women and children would line the streets.

"Let's go watch," Tom said.

"O.K.," I said. I tried to find our waiter, but he had joined the protesters. I dropped some money on the table, and Tom and I followed the mass exodus of women and children from the park. We stood behind the throng and watched over their heads as the all-male parade approached. Everyone seemed liberated by this new configuration; even the band sounded less rinky-dink.

The second parade was followed by a series of patriotic speeches, but as the evening waned the mood of the crowd mellowed: The schoolchildren were sent home to bed and the band began to play pop music. Couples danced on the plaza.

Tom and I were sitting on a bench near the fountain, watching the dancing, drinking beer from cold gold bottles. It had gotten late and we were exhausted, but there was something pleasurably transporting about being in the park. One felt successfully and completely in a foreign country, that one could return home and say, "One night there was a political rally in the public gardens . . ."

"I want to dance," said Tom.

"We can't dance," I said. "It's not a good idea."

"Of course it's not a good idea," said Tom. "Forget the idea. Come dance. Over there, where it's dark."

"No," I said. "It's dangerous."

"Everyone's drunk," said Tom. "They won't notice." He stood up and pulled me from the bench. We pressed through the swoon of dancing couples; everyone did seem drunk and self-intent. We made it to the other side of the park, away from the lights and the band, but even there it was obviously too public. Tom crossed the street and walked down a dirt alley. I followed him behind the buildings into a small enclosed parking lot crowded with pickup trucks. We sidled between them until we came to a place in the center where we were surrounded on all sides by trucks. None of the trucks had wheels, I noticed. The music from the park was faint yet audible. We stood for a moment, facing each other.

"Do you want to dance?" I asked.

"No," said Tom.

"Then what are we doing here?"

"I don't know," said Tom.

"Let's go back," I said.

"Wait," said Tom. He was picking rusted paint off the door of a truck. I stilled his hand with my own. I remembered them touching underwater at the fish cave. This time our hands were both hot, and I could feel his hand. I held it against the truck, but he pulled it away.

"Do you love Albert?" he asked.

"What makes you think that?"

"Just answer," he said.

"I don't know," I said. "I don't think so."

"But you've slept with him," said Tom.

"Yes," I said. "How did you know?"

"Irene told me," said Tom.

For a moment I had to think of who Irene was. And then I remembered the moment Tom and Irene reappeared on the veranda, how we had all stopped talking for a moment. I felt a little woozy so I sat down on the truck's running board. It had been Albert's idea to have Tom to dinner: He had told me not having dinner would have been childish, uncivilized.

"She told me when we went upstairs," Tom was saying. "While we were looking at her gold snuffboxes. At first I thought she was crazy. She thought I knew all about it."

"I'm sorry," I said.

"About what?"

"That I didn't tell you myself. It's just that, well, I didn't tell you because it's not a big deal."

"It's not?" asked Tom.

"No," I said.

"Is anything a big deal to you?"

"Yes," I said. "Of course."

"What?" asked Tom.

I tried to think of what was a big deal, but nothing came to mind, so I didn't answer. We were both quiet for a moment. The band seemed suddenly loud, but then I realized it wasn't the band but a sort of rickety explosion. Fireworks, I thought. I actually looked up at the sky, watching for their bright and sudden unblossoming, but the noise continued and the sky remained dark. And then the noise stopped, and I could hear the people on the plaza screaming.

As I entered my apartment the next afternoon the phone was ringing. I knew it would be Albert, and I let it ring, for I wanted to know how long Albert would wait. I stood and listened to it ring, not counting, just listening. It rang a very long time before I picked it up.

"Hello," I said.

"You're back," said Albert. "Thank God. I was worried. I heard about the violence. Are you all right?"

"Yes," I said.

"Were you at the rally? I heard there were a lot of foreigners there."

"We had just left. We were across the street, in a parking lot."

"What were you doing there?"

"Nothing. Tom wanted to dance."

"He wanted to what?"

"Dance," I said. "Everyone was dancing."

"Not for long, poor things," said Albert. "Well, thank God you're safe. Are you heading south?"

"No," I said. "Tom's gone back."

"Has he?"

"Yes," I said. "It was difficult."

"It often is," said Albert. "Well, I can't say I'm sorry. So you're alone?"

"Yes," I said.

"Are you going in to work?"

"No."

"I could come over."

"No," I said.

"What about dinner?" asked Albert. "We could have a nice dinner."

"No," I said.

"My, what a lot of no's," said Albert. He paused. "Nothing's changed, has it?"

I didn't answer.

"You must be exhausted," said Albert. "Have a stiff drink and go to bed. I'll call you later."

He hung up. So did I. I looked around the room. Tom's dress shoes stood by the terrace doors. By departing so hurriedly, he had left some of his things behind. That morning we had flown from Kunda to the capital; Tom changed planes and flew directly home. We had said good-bye in THE MEETING AND GREETING AREA. In the country to which I had been posted, leaving, saying good-bye, hadn't yet been officially sanctioned.

PART III

See, now we two together must bear
piece-work and parts as though it were the whole.
Helping you will be hard. Above all, do not
Plant me in your heart. I should grow too fast.

—RAINER MARIA RILKE, "SONNETS TO ORPHEUS" (I, 16)

PART III.

THE HALF
YOU DON'T KNOW

Miss Alice Paul was in a quandary. Ever since Rose had died, everything had gone wrong. And it wasn't getting better—it had been a month already, but it was no better. It was worse, she thought: much worse. Right this minute, Rose's grandson, a man named Knight, was up in the attic going through Rose's things, and there was nothing she could do about it. She stood in the upstairs hall, clutching the folding stairs that had collapsed from the ceiling. She had tried to climb them, but she couldn't. She had trouble enough getting up the regular stairs.

The problem was, nobody was telling her anything. It looked like they were moving Rose's stuff out of the house, or maybe Knight was moving in? Miss Alice Paul had lived in this house for about twenty years, ever since she met Rose at the Del Ray Luncheonette counter. They were both eating BLTs on white toast. It had made perfect sense for them to move in together—Rose was widowed and Miss Alice Paul was the tragic victim of a brief, annulled and (she hoped) forgotten marriage, but now that Rose was dead it turned out the house was really her daughter's, and nobody was talking about what would become of her. It was just too awful for words.

"Knight?" Alice Paul called up the stairs. He had a radio going up there. "Knight!" She shouted louder.

He turned the radio down. Good. "Yes?" he said.

"Are you sure I can't help with that? What are you doing?"

"Just going through this stuff. It's mostly junk, Miss Paul. I don't know the last time anyone's been up here."

"Yes, but what are you going to do with it?"

"Well, throw it out, most likely."

"Oh, dear. You don't suppose I could see it first? I mean, there might be something that was special to me, something you'd overlook."

"Well, sure you can see it. I have to bring it all down anyway. You can look through it then."

Well, that was a relief. God only knew what was up there, and what that boy might throw away. "Would you like a cold drink or something? Is it hot up there?"

But there was no answer. He had turned the radio back up. Miss Alice Paul went downstairs to the kitchen. She made a cup of tea and then put on her coat and went outside. It was a sunny day, mild for November, and she had read that sunlight can cure depression, so she was trying to sit outside whenever possible.

Deirdre Kassbaum was hanging out her wash next door. Or no, she was taking it down, folding it. Miss Alice Paul walked over to the fence.

"Do you need some help?" she asked.

Deirdre took a clothespin out of her mouth. "Oh, hi, Miss Paul."

Miss Paul repeated her offer.

"No thanks. I'm just going to finish these off in the dryer. They're still kind of damp."

"It's a nice day for air drying," Alice Paul said. Maybe I could go live with the Kassbaums, she thought. They've got that whole upstairs they never use. I could rent a room. Mr. Kassbaum drinks, but he's not a mean drunk.

"I see Knight's here," Mrs. Kassbaum said. "Is that his truck?"

"No. He rented it."

"Is he moving you out?"

"No," said Miss Alice Paul. She was trying to think how much people rented rooms for nowadays. The last time she rented a room, it was twelve dollars a week. Double that: twenty-five dollars—would that be enough? "I mean I don't know. I don't know what's going to happen."

"Well, are they selling the house?" Mrs. Kassbaum left the laundry basket on the lawn and walked over to the fence.

"I don't know," said Miss Alice Paul. "They won't tell me anything. It's driving me crazy."

"Well, that's a shame. But you shouldn't get all worried. I'm sure it'll work out just fine. Plus, you've got your rights. They can't just kick you out after twenty-two years. It's a thing called squatting, squatter's rights. They had an article about it in the *Digest*. Not that they'd kick you out. But you got to find out what's going on. She left the house to Knight?"

"Well, not really. Her daughter up in Norwell owns it. She was renting it to Rose."

"Well, can't she rent it to you?"

"I doubt I can afford it. I'll probably have to rent a room someplace."

"Oh, you don't want to do that. Rent a room? Living with strangers, sharing a bathroom. That's would be so depressing, don't you think?" Mrs. Kassbaum patted Miss Paul's arm. "What you have to do, honey, is talk to him, find out what they're planning. Knight's a nice man. You know that. Go in and talk to him, and put your mind at rest."

Miss Paul turned around and looked back at the house. She could hear the radio coming out of the open attic window. The sun had gone around to the front, leaving the backyard in shadow. I missed the sun, she thought. It would be shining in the living room window now, creating a familiar pattern on the rug and the couch. If Rose were alive she would put down the blinds, so the sun wouldn't fade the upholstery.

*　　*　　*

Miss Alice Paul was trying to check her pocketbook under the table without Knight seeing her. They were sitting at a booth in the Casa Adobe, a Mexican restaurant, and Miss Alice Paul wasn't sure who was paying. Knight was the one who had suggested going out to dinner, and before she could think of an excuse not to he had her in the car. She was pretty sure she had a five-dollar bill, so she had ordered a taco plate, which was the cheapest thing on the menu, even though she had no idea what a taco was, but Knight had said that wasn't enough for dinner and had changed her order to a deluxe burrito platter—something she just knew she couldn't afford, let alone eat.

"You lose something?" Knight said. He was drinking a beer. He had peeled its foil collar back and was drinking it straight from the bottle. At a restaurant. Just imagine.

"I just want to be sure I have enough money," Miss Alice Paul said. "I don't want to have to do the dishes." She tried to laugh, but it didn't sound too good.

"Oh, forget that," Knight said. "This is my treat."

"Well, many thanks, but I couldn't allow that. Though it is sweet of you."

"Oh, come on." Knight reached across the table and grabbed her pocketbook from her hands, putting it on the seat beside him. "Now just relax," he said. "Are you sure you don't want a glass of wine? They have sangria, I think."

"No, thank you." Miss Alice Paul leaned back and tried to think straight. He's taken my bag, she thought. Good God. "Could I have my bag back?" she asked.

"Of course," said Knight. "On one condition."

"What's that?"

"On the condition that you don't open it until we get home. O.K.?"

"If you insist," Miss Alice Paul said.

"I do," said Knight. "I insist."

Their deluxe platters arrived. "Good Lord," said Miss Paul. She couldn't help it. It just looked such a mess.

"Dig in," said Knight.

"I thought we'd have Thanksgiving at the house," Knight said. They were driving home from the restaurant, through a part of town Miss Alice Paul didn't seem to recognize. I don't get out much anymore, she thought. Everything's changing.

"What house?" she said.

"Your house," Knight said. "At Aunt Gran's." Aunt Gran was what they called Rose. She had never figured out why. Everyone in their family had pointless, misleading, disrespectful names: Rose's sixty-year-old daughter was called Topsy, and her daughter—Knight's sister—was sometimes called Ellen and sometimes called Nina, and Ellen's two children were called Kittery and Dominick. Hardly American names. She made sure they all called her Miss Alice Paul.

"There's more room there, and it's stupid to go back and forth from the lake. Is that O.K.?"

Miss Alice Paul was confused. What did he mean? He said *your house.* And who all was coming? "Who's coming?" she said.

"Topsy, and Ellen and Kittery and Dominick. They're coming down for the weekend. I figure the women can stay with you, and Dominick can stay with me. Or sleep on the couch. I don't know."

"I didn't buy a turkey." Was she supposed to do all the cooking? She hadn't cooked a turkey in years. Decades.

"No. Topsy said she was bringing one. And I'm making pies. You don't have to worry about anything." He pulled into a gas station. It was self-serve. "Excuse me," he said, before getting out.

Excuse me. He's a nice man, Miss Alice Paul told herself. He has manners, and he's quiet and he was listening to classical music on the radio. He was a professor at the university. He taught history or something. For a while he had lived with another professor, a man named John, who had sometimes come to Sunday dinner, but John had been killed about two years ago. His car cracked up, driving out to the lake in the winter. All that ice. Had he been drunk? Most men drink. Hector Kassbaum. Knight drinking that beer from the bottle. Disgusting. She watched him pump the gas. He was trying to get the numbers even, pumping little spurts. He paid the girl, and got back into the car.

In the driveway she realized she had forgotten to leave any lights on. Rose always left the porch light on, and one in the living room. It was strange to see the house so dark. Like nobody lived in it. She sat there for a moment.

"Want me to come in with you?" Knight said.

"Would you?" Miss Alice Paul asked. "Just for a minute."

"Sure," he said. He opened his door and came around and opened hers.

He held her elbow going up the front walk. "I should have left a light on," she said. "Rose always did. I forgot."

He grunted. He was looking up at the sky. She looked up, too. It was filled with stars. She felt dizzy looking up, and leaned closer to him.

"It's dark," he said. "Careful."

I'll ask him when we get inside, she thought. I'll offer him some coffee—do I have any coffee?—and ask him what he meant when he said *your house.* He let go of her arm on the front step and opened the screen door. He reached in to open the front door, but it was locked. "Do you have keys?" he asked.

Did she? She forgot the door locked when she closed it. She didn't think she had keys. It was all his fault, making her go out to dinner, getting her agitated; she had forgotten all about the keys when she left. But maybe they were in her bag. "Let me see," she said. She opened her bag and tried to look, but it was too dark. She backed up into the moonlight and almost fell off the stoop. He grabbed her. "Woops," he said, taking her bag. "Let me look."

This was awful, she thought. He's going through my bag now.

He took out her change purse and her plastic rain hat and her tissues. He felt around with his big hand. "Nope," he said. He reassembled her purse and handed it to her. "You wait here," he said. "I'll go around back. I can get in through the cellar, I think."

He disappeared behind the house. She looked back up at the sky. Birds were flying around the edges of the trees. Were they bats? They sure flew funny—jerky and silent. Don't look at them, she thought. Just stand here. Don't think of anything.

She waited what seemed like a long time. Then a light came on in the living room, and the front door opened. "Come in," he said. But something had changed. It was him inside first. It made it different.

"Come in," he repeated. He opened the screen door wider. He snapped on the porch light. "Oh, no," he said, when he saw her face. "What's the matter? Miss Paul?"

Am I crying? she wondered. I must be. That must be it.

Rose's daughter Topsy was washing the dishes, and Miss Alice Paul was drying and putting away, supposedly because she knew where things went. But she didn't. Half this stuff she had never seen before, so she just put things where she could find space. She'd sort it out later. After they all left tomorrow.

"It's nice to have a little peace and quiet for a change," said Topsy. "I hope this weekend wasn't too hectic for you."

"Oh, no," Miss Paul said, thinking, It will be peace and quiet when you're gone. Actually it hadn't been that bad. They were nice people even if there were too many of them. And they all shouted a lot. Tonight everyone had gone to the movies. They tried to make her go, but she just hated the movies. All that filthy language.

"Well, I'm glad we have this chance to talk, Miss Paul. There's something we have to discuss." Topsy had finished washing the dishes. She chased the suds down the drain and turned the faucet off.

Miss Alice Paul was drying the pronged bulbous foot of the electric mixer. She drew the towel back and forth between its curves. For some reason she couldn't stop. Finally the towel got all tangled up and Topsy took it away from her.

"Let's sit down," she said. "The rest of this can dry overnight." They sat at the table. "I was wondering if you had thought about where you might like to live, now that Rose is gone. As you probably know, we're planning to rent this house starting the first of the year."

"I didn't know," said Miss Alice Paul.

"Well, this old house is too big for you, anyway. It's too big for any one person."

"How much are you renting it for?"

"We're going to ask six hundred dollars a month."

That was highway robbery, thought Miss Paul. She's lying to me. "I doubt you'll find anyone willing to pay that," she said.

"In fact, we already have. That's why we have to talk. Do you have any relatives, Miss Paul, or friends, who could . . ."

"Everybody's dead. You might as well take me out into the street and drive the car right over me. That's what you should do."

"Don't talk crazy, now, Miss Paul. There are plenty of solutions. Knight tells me there's a real nice . . . place out by the lake. Have you ever heard of St. Luke's?"

St. Luke's was the rest home out by the lake. The very idea. "Course I have. But that's for—I'm not going to St. Luke's. I used to be a volunteer at St. Luke's. It's not a place for decent people. It's trash out there."

"Knight tells me it's real nice. I was thinking maybe we could drive out there tomorrow and have a look. I think they've fixed it up real nice since you—"

"You don't understand," said Miss Alice Paul. "I don't care if they got the Taj Mahal out there."

"Well, I don't think I can promise you the Taj Mahal, but what say we go take a look? It can't hurt to look, can it?"

People are just awful, Miss Alice Paul thought.

"So what do you say, Miss Paul? Let's go take a look."

"No," said Miss Alice Paul.

"Oh, come on, Miss Paul. It won't hurt you to look. Can't you do that much? We're just trying to help you, remember."

"No. I'm sorry, but no. Just no."

"Well," said Topsy. "I think that's a shame. I think you could be real happy out there."

"No," said Miss Alice Paul.

Kittery, the girl, Rose's great-granddaughter, was giving Miss Alice Paul a facial. Miss Alice Paul was sitting on a chair pushed away from the kitchen table, a plastic produce bag stuck on her head to hold her hair back. She was smiling—things had worked out as well as they could. At Christmas they had moved her up north to Norwell. They had a big old house—the biggest house she had ever seen. There was one whole floor they didn't even use.

Kittery was rubbing a peach-colored cream into her cheeks. It felt good. "This is apricot," she said. "It's really for younger skin, I think, like teenagers, but we'll just keep it on for a minute. It's got ground-up apricot. Wait till you see your glow!" Kittery had a job selling this stuff door-to-door. She also had a boyfriend who was a black man.

Dominick came in from the front hall.

"Hi," said Kittery.

Dominick said hi and opened the refrigerator. He was her favorite. They played gin rummy sometimes.

"How are you, Dominick?" she asked.

"I'm cold."

"Then shut the refrigerator," said Kittery.

Dominick shut it but continued to regard it.

"I'm thirsty," he announced. "What are we having for dinner?"

"You're on your own," Kittery said. "Topsy's spending the night at Knox Farm, and Ellen's at dance class." Ellen was their mother. She was plain nuts.

"Why's Topsy staying over there?"

"She said she had a lot to do and didn't want to drive home in the snow. I'm fasting. I heard on the radio that today is a national fast day. I'm starting now. Actually about an hour ago."

"What about Miss Alice Paul?" Dominick reopened the refrigerator. He took out a carton of orange juice.

"Well, you might fix her something when you make your own dinner. Are you hungry, Miss Alice Paul?"

"Vaguely," said Miss Alice Paul.

"I could make an omelet," said Dominick. "We learned how today in home ec. Do we have an omelet pan?"

"It's stinging," said Miss Alice Paul. "Is it supposed to sting?"

"Yes," said Kittery. "That means it's penetrating the epidermis."

"Do you want an omelet?"

"What kind?" asked Kittery.

"I was asking Miss Paul. I thought you were fasting."

"I think you're supposed to start in the morning. I'll do it tomorrow. Do you want an omelet, Miss Alice Paul? When we're done with your facial?"

"This is stinging like the dickens."

"We'll rinse it off. You got to put your head down between your legs, though, so the blood will rush to your face. That's a Lottie Dale secret. That's how you get the glow."

Everyone at the senior citizen nutrition lunch was pretending that noon was really midnight, and they were going to count down and then blow their horns and celebrate the New Year. They had to have their lunch—beef stew—an hour earlier today, at eleven o'clock. Miss Alice Paul hated coming to nutrition lunches. Topsy made her. She said it was good for her to get out of the house.

Miss Alice Paul had taken off her party hat twice, and both times Pauline Carlson had come round and told her to put it back on.

"Miss Alice Paul, don't be a party pooper," she said. "Let's cooperate. If one person takes their hat off, everyone will want to."

"So let them," Miss Alice Paul said.

"What kind of party would that be?" Pauline said. She put the hat—which looked like toilet paper rolls covered in tin foil—back on Miss Alice Paul's head and adjusted the elastic under her chin. Miss Alice Paul felt self-conscious because she knew she hadn't plucked all her whiskers that morning. She couldn't find her tweezers. The girl had stolen them, she was pretty sure.

A woman dressed up as the Statue of Liberty was coming around with Dixie cups filled with ginger ale. "Save this for the toast," she said, every time she put a cup on someone's tray. "Don't drink it yet."

The woman on Miss Alice Paul's left had fallen asleep, and the woman on her right didn't speak English. God only knew what she spoke—gobbledygook, it sounded like.

Miss Alice Paul got up to go to the bathroom.

"Where are you going?" Mrs. Carlson asked.

"To the ladies' room."

"Do you want someone to go with you?"

"No," said Miss Alice Paul.

"Well, hurry back. We don't want you to miss the countdown."

In the bathroom Miss Alice Paul unhitched her garter belt; she thought that pantyhose were somehow morally inferior to stockings. It was nice and quiet. She could hear them counting down outside. The fools. She covered the seat with toilet paper and sat on it, hearing the roar of noon in the cafeteria. Then she urinated as hard as she could, trying to block out their noise with her own.

When the senior citizens had successfully toasted the New Year, Mrs. Carlson closed the shades and dimmed the lights. She clapped her hands for silence and, being the type of woman she was, got it. "Happy New Year!" she shouted, and raised both her arms above her head as if she were a successful political candidate. "Well, we have a special New Year's treat for you. Something nice and romantic and beautiful to watch. I'm happy to introduce Dillon and Deanne, from the Tuxedo Dance Academy, who are going to entertain us with some ballroom dancing."

Dillon and Deanne squeezed through the jungle of tables and wheelchairs and stood in a clearing in the middle of the cafeteria. They smiled and waved to the senior citizens. "Music, maestro," Dillon said, none too enthusiastically.

Mrs. Carlson lowered the needle to a record on the phonograph, which began playing at the wrong speed. Dillon and Deanne laughed and boogied frenetically for a moment, and then began to waltz as the speed was adjusted and the tune of "Auld Lang Syne" became recognizable.

Miss Alice Paul returned from the bathroom to find the cafeteria dark and rearranged. She couldn't find her seat so she stood against the wall. It was snowing out. Two people were dancing in the middle of the room. Miss Alice Paul recognized the woman from the bathroom. She had come in and changed—from a nylon snow suit into a ball gown. She had asked Miss Alice Paul to zip her up. Miss Alice Paul thought she had seen a tattoo on her back, but she could have been mistaken.

They finished dancing; some people applauded. Several in the group had fallen asleep. People always fell asleep when they turned the lights out. That was why they didn't show movies anymore.

"Well," Mrs. Carlson announced, breathlessly, as if she had been dancing herself, "wasn't that beautiful? Poetry in motion, is what I call it! Guess what? Dillon and Deanne have offered to dance with some of us! Let's show them how agile we are. Who'd like to dance?"

Miss Alice Paul was looking out at the snow falling in the

parking lot. A bus drew up to the curb and collected a line of people. She was wondering where the bus was going when Dillon appeared at her side and asked her to dance. For a moment she was confused—the snow had been falling with a disorienting richness, like fabric disintegrating in the sky—but then the lights dimmed again and Dillon led her through the tables, and she thought, Do I remember how to dance? She found she did: The motions were all still there somewhere, and she moved closer to Dillon and closed her eyes, which helped. She heard Dillon say "You're good," and she felt herself squeezing his arm, a strange, involuntary gesture, and her hand felt the shape of his biceps beneath his coat and held it and Dillon said "Let's try something," and he began to dance more intricately and Miss Alice Paul followed him, her feet articulating a language she thought she had forgotten, and for the first time in ages, she realized she knew what she was doing and she couldn't help laughing a little and Dillon said "Let's dip," and they did; they dipped, and when Miss Alice Paul opened her eyes she found that she and Dillon were the only ones dancing and that everyone was watching them.

No one realized Miss Alice Paul had bolted till Knight called on New Year's Eve, saying she had been picked up at the Bloomington bus station for loitering. Apparently she had gotten on a bus after the nutrition lunch and took it all the way to Bloomington, but once she got there she didn't know what to do. The police found her crying in the station.

No one ever did figure out what exactly had happened, because Miss Alice Paul stopped talking. She also kept her eyes closed most of the time after she came back to Norwell, squeezed tight, as if every moment were a scary scene in a movie.

At first everyone thought she was just mad at them and not talking out of spite, but after a few weeks, when she still hadn't said anything, Topsy called Carleen Dempster, the therapist at the

Norwell Mental Health Center. Carleen told Topsy to bring Miss Alice Paul in for a visit, but Miss Alice Paul wouldn't go. She just shook her head when Topsy suggested they go see a friend.

So Carleen made a house call, one night after dinner. While Dominick loaded the dishwasher, Topsy filled her in.

"Now, is she a relation of yours?" Carleen asked. She took out a little spiral notebook and wrote "Miss Alice Paul" on the top of a page.

"No," said Topsy. "She was a friend of my mother's."

"And now she's living with you?"

"Well, when my mother died, there was no place else for her to go. They lived together for about thirty years."

"Doesn't she have family?"

"No."

"Well, now, does she pay rent?"

"No," said Topsy. "She doesn't have any money."

"She has no income? What about Social Security?"

"She doesn't get any."

"What about welfare?"

"No," said Topsy. "She's just an old gentlewoman. She never worked. She was a pink lady for a while, I think, but that's volunteer."

"And she didn't pay rent when she lived with your mother?"

"I don't think so."

"But you're not sure?"

"She just helped out," said Topsy.

"Doing what?"

"I don't know. With the cooking and cleaning, I suppose."

"And she wasn't paid?"

"She wasn't an employee. She was a friend."

"And what about your mother's estate?"

"What about it?"

"Was this Miss Paul recognized by the estate?"

"No, this Miss Paul wasn't."

"So now she's just living off the goodness of your heart?"

"Yes, although she doesn't quite see it that way. She wanted to stay down in Bloomington, in my mother's house. Actually, it belongs to me. I was renting it to my mother."

"And you couldn't rent it to Miss Paul?"

"Like I said, she hasn't got any money."

"Well, who buys her clothes and all?"

"I don't know. She has things. They're all about a hundred years old. I bought her a new winter coat, but she doesn't wear it."

"Well, this sounds real complicated. She should have been on welfare all along. She must have some money coming to her."

"Well, I told you, she stopped talking. Ever since she came back from Bloomington."

"When did she go to Bloomington?"

"Over New Year's."

"And she hasn't talked since then?"

"No. At least not to me."

"She talked to me," said Dominick. He closed the dishwasher.

"Did she?" asked Topsy. "When?"

"The other night."

"What'd she say?" asked Carleen.

"Well, it was . . . I don't know if I should tell you."

"'Course you should," said Topsy. "Why not?"

"She's real sad," said Dominick. "She said she wanted to die. She asked me to run her over with the car."

"Oh, she asked me that, too," said Topsy. "I think that's just a ploy for sympathy."

"Well, you can't be too sure," said Carleen. "How old is she?"

"Well, I'm not sure. My mother was eighty-three, and Miss Alice Paul was about the same age. About that, I'd say."

"And do you want her to continue living here?"

"What do you mean? What can we do?"

"Well, maybe she should be at Heritage Hills."

"I don't think she'd like that," Topsy said.

"Well, let's ask her," said Carleen. "Where is she?"

"She's upstairs. She goes right up after dinner, sits in the dark. It's like she doesn't want to be here at all. Like she just wants to ignore everything."

"Dear oh dear," said Carleen. She followed Topsy up the back stairs. The door to Miss Alice Paul's room was closed. Topsy knocked.

"She won't say 'Come in,' or anything," Topsy said. She opened the door.

Miss Alice Paul was sitting on the bed, one hand braced on either side of her. The room was dark except for some stripes from the porch light. Topsy turned on the overhead light.

"Miss Alice Paul, this is the woman I was telling you about who wants to help you," Topsy said. "Her name is Mrs. Dempster."

Miss Alice Paul sat perfectly still, her eyes closed. Carleen walked over and put one of her hands on top of one of Miss Alice Paul's. Miss Alice Paul drew hers away.

"Hi, Miss Paul," Carleen said. "I'm real glad to meet you."

"Maybe I'll just leave you two alone," Topsy said.

"That'd be just great," said Carleen. "I'll be down in a while."

When Topsy had retreated Carleen turned the light off. "We'll just sit here in the dark," she said. "We don't need that old light, do we? I always did like to sit in the dark. It's real comforting." She sat down on the bed next to Miss Alice Paul and for a while she didn't say anything.

"What a real nice quilt this is," she finally said. "Did you make it?"

Miss Alice Paul didn't respond.

"I took a quilting class at Adult School a couple years ago, but all we ever made were pillows. Mine came out all lumpy. You need such patience to be a good quilter. It's a dying art, you know. It is for sure. 'Cause you see, it was women who did it, and now they're just all doing something else." She paused. "I mean, they all have jobs or something. I like my job, but sometimes I think it would be nice to have the time to do more things with my hands, things like quilting. Or just plain sewing."

Miss Alice Paul seemed to have relaxed a little. It was hard to tell.

"Miss Paul, I don't want to tell you what to do. I mean, I respect you, and if you don't want to talk to me, well, I think that's fine. I mean that. It's fine. But I think you should. I think you should talk to me because I can help you. And things aren't going to get better unless someone helps you. They're going to get worse."

She paused and put her hand back on top of Miss Alice Paul's. Miss Paul folded her hands in her lap. "You don't know the half of it," she said.

"What?" said Carleen. "Excuse me?"

Miss Alice Paul cleared her throat. "I was married once," she said. "And I'm not a widow and I'm not a wife and I'm not a divorcée."

Carleen thought it would be impolite to ask what indeed she was, even though Miss Alice Paul seemed to be waiting for that exact question.

"My marriage was annulled," Miss Alice Paul said. "It was annulled by the court and the Church after twenty-eight days."

"Well, huh," said Carleen, with great interest. And then, when Miss Alice Paul failed to continue she asked, "Why was it annulled?"

"I got married to Thomas Oliver Lippincott, which was not, of course, his real name. He had another wife. She was in a sanatorium up in Saranac, New York. He thought she was going to die of tuberculosis, but she did not die of tuberculosis."

"She got better?" Carleen asked.

Miss Alice Paul nodded her head, once, with vehemence.

"Miss Paul?" Carleen asked.

Miss Alice Paul stood and walked over to her dresser. She took a pin from her pin cushion, which was shaped like a gigantic mutant strawberry. She held it out in the dark, something shiny in her palm, for Carleen to see. "Sara Teasdale gave me this pin," she said. "Do you know of Sara Teasdale?"

"I don't think I do," said Carleen.

"Sara Teasdale was a poet. I met her in New York City, and I admired her brooch, and she gave it to me. She took it off her coat and gave it to me. It's made of agate and amber. She took it off her coat and said, "If you like it, please do have it.""

"Wow," said Carleen. "How interesting."

"Do you like it?" Miss Alice Paul asked. She walked back over to the bed, her arm outstretched, and stopped when her hand was in a patch of stray porchlight. A fat bumblebee rested in her palm.

"It's very pretty," said Carleen. "But I don't really wear—"

"Here," said Miss Alice Paul. "If you like it, please do have it."

The girl didn't take the pin. She left it on Miss Alice Paul's dresser. It looked as if it had been flying around the room and landed there. For a moment Miss Alice Paul tried to believe it was a real bee, that she was afraid of it. Then she picked it up and clutched it in her palm. The metal wings bit into her skin, but it wasn't like holding an object. It was like holding a feeling. This is pain, Miss Alice Paul thought. The harder she clutched it, the better it felt.

After a minute she opened her hand to see if her palm was bleeding, but it wasn't. There were just lines, red and calligraphic, like a Chinese character.

"There's a magician in the solarium," the girl said. "How does that sound?"

"What?" asked Miss Alice Paul.

"This afternoon's event is MAGIC. Do you want to go down to the solarium for a magic show?"

"I don't believe in magic," said Miss Alice Paul. "It's all just tricks."

"But they're fun to watch," the girl said. "Don't you think?"

"Why don't you go," suggested Miss Alice Paul, "and tell me all about it?"

"I think you're supposed to go," said the girl. "Your chart says you can go to all events."

"Does it say I must go? Is this Russia?"

"I guess you don't have to. I'll put down you were asleep."

"Don't lie on my account," said Miss Alice Paul. "I can't have that on my conscience."

"Why don't you just come down for a little while? If you don't like it, I'll bring you back up. I promise."

"What's your name?" asked Miss Alice Paul.

"Jane," said the girl.

"All right, Jane," said Miss Alice Paul. "I surrender."

"Good. I should think you'd like to get out of this room."

Miss Alice Paul looked around her hospital room. Since she had broken her ankle, she had been moved from The Lodge, the nicest building in Heritage Hills, into the intermediate care pavilion. She should never have tried to escape out the window at night. Not that she believed her ankle was really broken—she had walked to have it x-rayed. She was sure they had put a cast on her leg and her in a wheelchair and moved her to intermediate care only to keep her immobilized.

The solarium was not accurately named. It was illuminated not by the sun but by long tubes of fluorescent lights. The couches and chairs had, like their inhabitants, found their way to the solarium after what appeared to be long and taxing lives.

The magician, a lady in a green velvet tuxedo, was pouring water into a handkerchief folded to resemble a vase. When the pitcher was empty, she snapped the handkerchief open, revealing nothing but air. She paused for applause, but received none.

Her next trick required a volunteer, and she was vainly seeking one when Jane appeared beside Miss Alice Paul's wheelchair. "You've got a visitor," she said.

"A visitor?" asked Miss Alice Paul. "Who?"

"A friend," said Jane. "A boy. He's waiting in your room. I'll bring you up."

It was a boy: the boy. He was standing by the window, looking out, when Miss Alice Paul was wheeled in.

"I'll leave you two alone," Jane said. "Have a nice visit."

"Hi, Miss Alice Paul," the boy said. "Remember me?"

"Of course," she said. But she couldn't think of his name. He was just the boy. There had been the boy, and the girl, and the two ladies. The crazy one and the mean one. She had always liked the boy the best.

"I'm Dominick," he said, as if he knew she didn't know his name.

"Of course, Dominick," Miss Alice Paul said. "It's nice of you to come. Sit down."

He went to sit on her bed but then he noticed the bars were up, so he sat on the windowsill. He nodded out the window. "I was outside cutting the grass and I thought I'd come in and see you. See how you are. I haven't seen you in a while."

"No," said Miss Alice Paul.

"What happened to your foot?"

"They tell me it's broken."

"How did it happen?"

"An accident," said Miss Alice Paul.

"Does it hurt?"

"I don't feel it," said Miss Alice Paul. She looked at her foot, which was extended straight out in front of her, like a sword. She had forgotten about her feet. They were so far away from the rest of her. She had lost interest in them. Every other Thursday, she was lined up with the other residents, barefoot, in the corridor, and a podiatrist, who sat on a little rolling platform, scooted down the row, his head bowed over their gnarled, naked feet, trimming their toenails. Like Jesus washing the apostles' feet.

"It took me a while to find you," Dominick said. "This is a big place."

"Well, I used to be over there." Miss Alice Paul started to wave toward The Lodge, but then she realized she had no idea where it was. "But they moved me because of my foot. It was nicer over there."

"Maybe you'll get moved back," Dominick said.

"Maybe," said Miss Alice Paul. "I doubt it."

"Oh," said Dominick. He sounded disappointed.

"How are you?" asked Miss Alice Paul. "You said you were cutting grass?"

"Yes," said Dominick. "I have a job cutting grass. All over the county."

"That sounds . . . interesting," Miss Alice Paul said.

"Not really," said Dominick. "But it's nice to be outdoors."

"How's school?" asked Miss Alice Paul.

"It's over. I graduated. I start college in the fall."

"Where are you going?"

"Indiana University. Bloomington."

"I used to live in Bloomington," said Miss Alice Paul.

"I know," said Dominick. "With Aunt Gran."

Rose. If only Rose hadn't died.

"What will you study?"

"I'm not sure."

"What do you want to do?" She almost added, when you grow up, but she stopped herself.

Dominick shrugged. "I don't know."

"How's your sister?"

"Good. At least I think. She moved to California."

"To be a movie star?"

"No," said Dominick.

"What does she want to do?"

"She's not sure," said Dominick.

What unmotivated children, Miss Alice Paul thought. They'll get nowhere.

"And your mother?" she asked, thinking, I'll ask about the mother, but I won't ask about the grandmother. I'll be damned if I ask after her.

"She's O.K." He stood up. "I should get back to work," he said. "I just wanted to stop by."

"It was very kind of you," said Miss Alice Paul. "I'm sorry I can't offer you anything to eat."

"That's O.K.," said Dominick. "I just had lunch."

"Well, it was so nice of you to come."

Dominick smiled. "It was nice to see you," he said. "I've been thinking about you." He paused in the door. "Maybe I'll come again, before I leave for school."

"Please do," said Miss Alice Paul. "If you find the time."

"Is there anything you need? I could maybe bring you something."

"Oh, no," said Miss Alice Paul. She gestured around her little room. "I have everything I need right here. I'm quite . . . fine. But thank you."

"So long," said Dominick. "Take care."

"Good-bye," said Miss Alice Paul. He went out into the hall, apparently the wrong way, because he reappeared, walking in the opposite direction. He smiled at her, waved, was gone.

After a moment she tried to move her chair over to the window so she could watch him come out the front. But the girl had put the brake on, and she couldn't release it. She pulled with all her might but it wouldn't budge. Damn it, she thought. Damn it to hell.

EVERYWHERE
AND NO PLACE

I was in the living room, twirling around, when the phone rang. I went into the kitchen and answered it. Everything kept spinning.

"Hello," I said.

"Is Kittery there?" Ellen, my mother, asked. Kittery was my older sister.

"No," I said. "She's over Duane's."

"I suppose she took her car?"

"She did," I said.

"Is Topsy back yet?" On Friday nights, Topsy, my grandmother, ran the fish-fry at the Methodist Church.

"Not yet," I said.

"Oh God," Ellen said. "Dominick."

"What? Where are you?"

"I'm at the pharmacy. I'm standing here at the pharmacy, talking on the pay phone. Virginia Doyle is inside trying on sunglasses. I think she's spying on me."

"So," I said.

"So, I can't do it," Ellen said. "I just can't do it."

"What?"

"I can't walk home. I can't walk home alone."

Last Friday night, on her way home from work—Ellen's a bank teller, and the bank's open till eight Friday nights—she claims she was attacked. She says there was a man in the woods along Cobble Road, calling her filthy names, throwing sticks and moss and bottle caps at her. She arrived home hysterical and limping. One of her heels had broken.

"Do you want me to come down?" I asked.

"Would you? Just this once. Next week it will be O.K."

"It will take me a while to walk down."

"That's O.K.," Ellen said. "I'll wait right here."

I've always been more comfortable with Topsy, my grandmother; Ellen didn't live with us until I was twelve, six years ago. She had a nervous breakdown when her husband died, when I was a baby. We all lived in New York City then. Ellen was a fashion model called Nina Night. This is all I know about my father: His name was Alexander Deen, he was rich, he was twenty-four when he married my mother and twenty-eight when he dived off the side of a boat into the Atlantic Ocean and never resurfaced. He had been drinking; it was a hot, sunny day in August. After he died my mother tried to kill herself. Kittery and I were sent back to Indiana to live with Topsy. Now Ellen went to the Mental Health Center once a week and took pills to stay "stable."

It took me about half an hour to walk downtown. Ellen was standing in the greeting card aisle of the pharmacy, looking at the cards.

"They have some real sweet cards, now," she said. "Look at this." She handed me a card: a photograph of a bowl of fruit. Inside was written "Thinking of You."

"Isn't that a nice card?" she asked. "Wouldn't it be nice to get that card from someone?"

"It's stupid," I said. "What's the fruit got to do with anything? It looks plastic."

Ellen looked at the picture more closely. "I don't think that's the point," she said. "Maybe I'll send this to John Calvin." John Calvin Starr was the man Ellen had been dating, on and off, ever since she moved back to Norwell.

"I'm sure John Calvin will like it, especially if you send it to him," I said.

She bought the card and we started home. Ellen walked real slowly, as if every step were taking her into alien turf. We walked up Growper Street, past the dark high school. Ellen opened her bag and took out a half-eaten bagel wrapped in a napkin.

"Did you have dinner?" she asked. "Want a bite?"

"Sure," I said. She held the bagel out, and I bit into it. It was hard and tasteless. "It's stale," I said.

"Why didn't you go cook with Topsy?" she asked.

"I didn't feel like it."

"I appreciate your walking me home. You must think it's silly."

"No," I said. "I understand."

We walked along in a comfortable, accustomed silence. Ellen started tearing the bagel into little pieces and dropping the crumbs in the gutter. When we turned onto Cobble Road, which had no houses and fewer street lights, I could feel her tense up. The bagel was gone, sowed behind us, and she began shredding the napkin.

"Did you prove O.K.?" I asked. Every night Ellen had to prove out at the bank—make sure the cash in her drawer was the right amount.

"Smack on the nose," she said, but she didn't sound happy about it. We were walking down the middle of the road, where the white line would have been had there been a white line. Our shadows kept waxing and waning as we moved from one street-light toward another, and I was concentrating on that pattern, trying to find the moment when the direction of our shadows changed, but there were a few dark steps in between the lights where they just disappeared.

Ellen stopped walking and pointed into the woods at some

dark trunks of trees beyond a low, disintegrating stone wall. "This is where it happened," she said.

"You thought someone was in there?" I asked.

She didn't answer. She stood in a pool of light, her shadow puddled beneath her, staring into the woods.

"There's no one in there," I said. I walked up the embankment and stood on the stone wall, picked up a small rock and threw it into the woods. It hardly made a sound, like it landed on a pillow. "See," I said. I turned around.

Ellen was still standing beneath the light, but she was swaying back and forth, as if she were being hypnotized.

"There's no one in there," I repeated.

"I know there's no one in there," Ellen said. "Of course there's no one in there. He's long gone by now."

Topsy always took a shower when she got back from the church dinner—"To wash the fish stink off." I was lying on the living room floor watching a movie on TV. Ellen had gone to bed.

Topsy came into the living room, pinning her long wet hair on top of her head. It looked black, but when it dried you could see it was really gray. She stood behind me, watching the TV for a minute. Then she jiggled my shoulder with her foot.

"Come on," she said.

"Where are we going?"

"On a mission. You and me. Come on."

"I'm watching this."

"I've never seen anything so stupid in my life," Topsy said. "Come on."

She wouldn't tell me where we were going. We got into the car and drove downtown, then out toward the sand pit. We stopped in front of Duane's mobile home. Duane was Kittery's boyfriend. He was a chemistry teacher and wrestling coach at Norwell High School. He was also thirty, and black.

Kittery had been seeing Duane since she was a junior in high school, three years ago. They had kept their romance pretty much a secret until Kittery graduated. Now they drive around town together, and Kittery spends as many nights at Duane's as she does at home. Topsy periodically has a "talk" with Kittery. She's always trying to get Kittery out of Norwell and back "on the right track." Kittery did go down to the University at Bloomington, but she only stayed for a semester. Now she sells Lottie Dale cosmetics, at least when she's in the mood.

Topsy and I got out of the car, walked up the metal steps, and knocked on the door. Duane opened it. He was wearing a T-shirt and gym shorts and white socks. Behind him Kittery lay on the couch, watching TV: the same movie I had been watching. Duane didn't say anything. He held the door open, turned around, and looked at Kittery.

"What are you guys doing here?" Kittery asked. She sat up, but continued watching the TV. Topsy ducked under Duane's arm. Duane stepped aside, and said, "Hi, Nick."

"Hi," I said. I followed my grandmother into the suddenly crowded mobile home. Topsy turned the TV off and stood in front of it, waiting for everybody to focus his attention on her. We all pretty much did.

"Would you like to go put some trousers on, Duane?" Topsy asked.

Duane looked down at his bare, muscular legs. "That's O.K.," he said.

"Well," Topsy sighed. "I don't know. I just don't know." There was a silence while we all considered this statement: Was she referring to Duane's naked legs?

"Don't know what?" prompted Kittery. She lay back down on the couch, her head in Duane's lap.

I was watching Topsy. I knew she had hoped to find Duane and Kittery involved in some illicit activity: gambling, hashish smoking, oral sex, anything but watching the same dumb movie that had been playing in her very own living room ten minutes ago. But the sight of Kittery's head in Duane's lap seemed to refuel her energies. She took a good long look at them and said, "Kittery, darling, just because you're young and smart and beautiful doesn't mean you can behave any way you want. Now you know me and your brother are worried sick about you. Aren't we, Dominick?"

I shook my head in an ambiguous sort of way. Kittery was trying not to laugh.

Topsy noted this, but continued. She was not easily thwarted. "Well, at least I am. Worried sick. What about you, Duane?"

"I don't think I am. Am I, Kittery?"

"Duane's not worried about me, Topsy," Kittery confirmed.

"Just look at you," Topsy said. "If you could only see yourself."

Kittery stood up. She was wearing sweatpants and a flannel shirt. They both belonged to Duane. If she wasn't so beautiful she would have looked awful. She took a deep breath and smiled. "I'm being a bad hostess, aren't I? Could I get you something to drink? Dominick?"

"Sure," I said.

"Why don't you come help me?" Kittery said. "We'll let Topsy and Duane talk."

Kittery and I went into the kitchen. Everything was miniature-sized. Kittery opened the back door. "Let's split," she said. "I'm not hanging around for this."

"What about Duane?"

"Duane's a big boy," Kittery said. "Duane can take care of himself."

Kittery was the only girl in the history of Norwell High School to be elected homecoming queen three years in a row, but she doesn't want to be a model. She thinks that's what messed Ellen up; she's convinced all those flashbulbs fry your brain cells. Kittery is so beautiful that Mr. Templer, of Templer Ford, gives her a free car every year. All she has to do is drive it in the Memorial Day Parade, wearing her prom gown, long white gloves, sunglasses, and a sash that says "There's a Ford in Your Future."

Kittery and I drove into town with the top down and radio turned up loud. We pulled into Ransom's. "Want to get a drink?" Kittery asked. She got free drinks at Ransom's.

"Sure," I said.

We went inside and sat at the bar. The movie we had both been watching was on the TV above it.

"I'm starving," I said. "I didn't have dinner."

"I thought you were going with Topsy."

"I didn't. I walked Ellen home."

"How'd she do?"

"She kind of freaked out for a while, but we made it."

"Jesus," Kittery said. She ordered a beer and I ordered a Coke and some french fried zucchini—a speciality of Ransom's. John Calvin appeared, holding a pool stick. John Calvin practically lived in Ransom's.

"Howdy," he said. He took one of my zucchinis.

"Hi, John Calvin," Kittery said. "You winning or losing?"

"I'm just killing time."

"I should call Duane," Kittery said. "Do you have a dime?"

Both John Calvin and I gave her a dime. She kept both of them, and went into the back to use the phone.

John Calvin took out a cigarette and lit it. "So what's new?" he asked.

"I've decided I'm going to be a ballet dancer," I said.

"A ballet dancer? Huh. What made you think of that?"

"We're learning it in school. I'm getting pretty good."

"You'll have to move someplace to do that," John Calvin said. "There's not much demand for ballet dancers around here."

"I'll move to Europe or something," I said.

"Kittery seems more like the one who should be a ballet dancer."

"Kittery's clumsy," I said. "Plus she's too tall. The woman can't be too tall, or they dwarf the men, when they stand up on their tippytoes."

"Huh," said John Calvin. "You're not serious about any of this, are you?"

"No."

"That's good. Otherwise, I'd worry about you."

Kittery returned. "Guess what?" she said. "Topsy ran over Rocky!"

"Is he dead?" I asked.

"Rocky? No. But he crawled under the house and won't come out. He's making strange noises. Duane wants me to pick up a can of tuna. You want a ride home?"

"Can you drop me at Elsa's?" Elsa was my girlfriend.

"Sure," said Kittery. "Good night, John Calvin. You want to finish my beer?"

Mrs. Ellwood, Elsa's mother, was standing at the dining room table, cutting out a pattern. I watched her for a moment through the screen door before I knocked. Johnny Carson was on the TV in the living room, but the sound was turned off. His guest was Barbara Eden.

Mrs. Ellwood looked up when I knocked, her mouth full of pins. She took them out and said, "Come on in, Dominick."

I opened the door and went inside.

"Elsa's out back," Mrs. Ellwood said. "Doing her insects."

"O.K.," I said. "What are you making?"

"The costumes for *Brigadoon*. The Jaycees are putting it on next month."

"What's *Brigadoon*?"

"It's a musical," said Mrs. Ellwood. "About Mary, Queen of Scots."

I went through the kitchen and out the back door. Elsa was standing under the grape arbor with a notebook, pen, and flashlight. For the science fair, she was doing a project about insects: charting a certain area of the backyard, checking it once during the day and once at night, recording all the insects she saw. My project involved coating teeth with different types of toothpaste, soaking them in Coca-Cola, and seeing which ones rotted first.

"Ssshh," Elsa said. "I've got some weird moth here." She bent into the grape arbor, her face disappearing among the leaves. "Where have you been, anyway?" she asked. "What time is it?"

"It's about midnight," I said. "I've been everywhere."

"I've been no place," said Elsa.

I walked across the lawn and stood beside her. She extracted her head from the vines. "Look at this," she said. She pointed her flashlight into the tumble of grape leaves at a powdery, blue-tinted moth.

"What kind of moth is that?" I asked.

"I don't know. I'll check the book. There are so many."

"It's kind of disgusting," I said. "All these insects."

"I think it's great," said Elsa. "It's wild. I've found some that aren't even in the book. They must be mutants or something. How are your teeth coming?"

"They're all rotting pretty good."

The moth batted its wings and flew up into the night, like a confused snowflake. I sat on the lawn. Elsa sat beside me, shining the flashlight at my face. Then she turned it off. "You smell like smoke," she said.

"I was in Ransom's," I said.

"Who with?"

"Kittery. And John Calvin."

"Watch," Elsa said. "I've been practicing. I can do it." She stood up and assumed first position. She began spinning around, pivoting off her feet, keeping her head forward and jerking it around at the very last second. Elsa and I were taking ballet for our gym elective that semester. Spotting is a technique dancers use so they don't get dizzy while they spin: They focus on one point, and turn their heads just once each spin. If you do it right, you can spin forever.

"Get up," Elsa said. "Let's see you do it."

I stood up. "I was practicing before," I said.

"Well, come on. Let's see," said Elsa. I started spinning but I couldn't find my focus point. I was going around too quickly. I got dizzier and dizzier. Finally I closed my eyes and just spun till I fell on the ground. I lay there with my eyes closed.

"You're hopeless," I heard Elsa say.

I didn't move. Even with my eyes closed, I could feel the starry sky swaying above me. Elsa lay down on top of me. She put her hands inside my shirt, touching the skin of my chest.

"I heard today," she said.

"Heard what?"

"From Princeton. I got in."

Elsa had applied early decision to Princeton.

"Wow," I said. "Congratulations."

"I wish you would go, too," she said.

"I'm going to Bloomington," I said. "I can't get into Princeton."

"You could try," said Elsa.

"You know I can't," I said.

I opened my eyes. I watched the stars swing slower and slower until they stopped.

"Well, in a way I envy you," I heard Elsa say. "IU's a good school. And you'll know people there. You'll have friends right from the start."

"Kittery hated it there. She said everyone was a moron. All they did was throw up, she said."

"Kittery's friends probably did. But you'll meet different people."

I didn't want to talk about college so I didn't say anything.

Elsa withdrew her hands and stood up. "Let's practice that thing. That lift thing where you pick me up. I heard that they might discontinue ballet because fifth period, Eric Bloor dropped Debbie Shaddock on her head. Stand up."

I stood up and put my hands on Elsa's small hips, lifted her up. She was thin, and I was strong. "O.K.," she said. "Twirl me."

On my way home I walked through town, and stopped back in Ransom's. It was pretty empty, but John Calvin was still there, sitting in a booth by himself. A green plastic cover lay over the pool table. It looked like a made bed.

John Calvin looked up at me. "Dominick," he said. "What are you still doing up?"

"It's Friday night," I said. I sat down across from him.

"That's true," John Calvin said. "Kittery's gone. She left about an hour ago."

"I know," I said. "I left with her."

"But you came back."

"I know."

"Kittery didn't," John Calvin said, as if he were winning an argument. He killed his beer and set it carefully in the middle of the table, on top of a carved heart. "I don't suppose you've got a car?"

"No," I said. "I'm walking home."

"I guess I am, too," John Calvin said. "I've been waiting for someone with a car to drive me home. But no luck."

"What happened to your car?"

"Nothing. My car's fine. I lost my license." He stood up, and put some money on the table. "Let's walk," he said.

John Calvin walked with one foot on the curb and one foot in the gutter, then got tired of it, and walked next to me on the sidewalk. He hummed. "What'd Ellen do tonight?" he asked after a while.

"She was in bed when I left. She's still a little spooked, I think. I had to walk her home."

"You walk a lot," John Calvin said.

I didn't answer.

"It was me," John Calvin said.

"What?"

"It was me in the woods," he said. "In case you hadn't figured."

"Oh," I said. "No."

"I was gonna surprise her. You know, just say BOO or something. Just surprise her. I was waiting in the woods, just standing there. She was walking so slow, and as she got near me, I realized she was singing. I never heard her sing. She was standing under the streetlight, singing, like she was on a stage or something."

"What was she singing?"

"I don't know," John Calvin said. He reverted to his awkward form of walking, his hands in his jeans pockets. "Some song. But something about it got me mad. It just irritated me, hearing her sing alone, like that. 'Cause she never sings. Did you ever hear her sing?"

"No," I said. "Well, at church, maybe."

"I just started throwing things at her. Not to hurt her, just to— hell, I don't know. Just to make her stop, I guess. I didn't yell names at her. She made that part up."

We were in front of the high school. Some cars were parked in the lot, with kids drinking beer in them. We could hear the music from their radios.

"Punks," John Calvin muttered. "I'm gonna cut through the football field," he said. "You think she knows it was me?"

"I don't know," I said. "I don't think so."

John Calvin shrugged. "Don't tell her, O.K.?"

I shook my head no.

John Calvin reached out and touched my shoulder. "I love her so much," he said. "Sometimes it makes me be crazy." He walked off across the football field.

I watched John Calvin disappear. A voice from the cars called me but I didn't answer; I walked to the end of the street and turned onto Cobble Road. I hadn't walked very far when Kittery pulled up beside me. The radio was playing loud. She turned it down a little.

"Finally," she said. "I've been looking all over for you."

"I've just been walking home," I said.

"Get in," she said.

"I think I want to walk," I said. I kind of wanted to be alone for a while.

"No," Kittery said. "I've got to talk to you. Get in."

I got into the car. Kittery drove up Cobble Road, past our house. There were lights on up on the third floor, which meant Topsy was wallpapering. No one lives on the third floor, but Topsy wallpapers the bedrooms up there when she can't sleep. "Topsy's wallpapering," I said.

"I bet she is," said Kittery.

"Where are we going?" I asked. We were driving out the Range Road, away from town. Kittery was speeding. She had her left arm extended out the window, cupping and uncupping the night. She didn't answer me. "What do you want to talk about?" I asked.

Kittery looked over at me. The car went off the road, onto the flat grassy range. Kittery just kept driving as if nothing had happened. When it started to get bumpy she slowed down, and parked under a tree. She turned the engine off. Suddenly it was very quiet.

"Duane and I are leaving," she said.

"What do you mean?" I asked.

"We're moving away," said Kittery. "Tonight."

"Tonight? Don't you think that's a little sudden?"

"There's nothing wrong with doing things suddenly," said Kittery. "It's better this way."

"Where are you moving?"

"We're not sure. Maybe someplace like Minnesota. Or Idaho. We're just going to drive until we find someplace we want to live."

"What made you decide this?"

"Well, we've been thinking about it for a while. We're both sick to death of Norwell. And after Topsy came over tonight, well, you know, in a way she's right, I mean, what am I doing here? Nothing. And then when Rocky died, well, Duane decided he just wanted to leave. If we don't leave tonight, we might never leave. So we're leaving tonight. I've been driving all over trying to find you. You're the only one we're telling."

"Rocky died?"

"Yes. Duane's burying him."

"Duane can't just leave in the middle of the night. He has a job."

"A job he can't stand."

"I think you're both crazy," I said.

"I was going to give you my car," said Kittery.

"Mr. Templer will want it back. He won't want me driving it around."

"Well, until he does. I'm leaving it at Duane's. There's a set of keys in my jewelry box at home."

"What happens if something happens? Like if you and Duane run out of money? Or can't find jobs?"

"There's always some job you can do. I can always sell Lottie Dale. And Duane can substitute teach."

"Not if he leaves his job here without giving notice."

"This will be in a different state," said Kittery. She started the car and drove it slowly back toward the road. "Why are you being so negative? I thought you'd be happy for me."

"I think you're crazy," I said.

"That's because you don't understand. Do you know what it's like being me in this town? Loving Duane? It's just a mess. And it's a mess for Duane, too."

"What makes you think it's going to be better someplace else?"

"It might not be better. But it will be different. It's always different someplace else," Kittery said. She stopped the car a ways from the house. "I'm going to drop you off here 'cause I don't want Topsy to see the car. I've had enough input from her tonight."

"Aren't you going to say good-bye to her?"

"No," said Kittery.

"What about Ellen?"

"I'm not going away forever," said Kittery. "I'm just moving."

"Is that what I should tell them?"

"Yes," said Kittery.

"Topsy will be worried," I said.

"That's nothing new," said Kittery.

I sat still for a moment. I knew Kittery wanted me to get out so she could go, but I didn't want her to go. I didn't want anyone to go anywhere. I tried to think of something to say. "It was John Calvin," I said.

"What?"

"In the woods, last week. Throwing stuff at Ellen."

"John Calvin did that?"

"That's what he told me. He said she was singing and it made him mad so he threw sticks at her."

"And you think I'm crazy for leaving this town," said Kittery. "I'd get out quick if I were you."

"I like it here," I said.

Kittery leaned over and kissed me. "I've got to go. Duane wants to leave. I'll call you in a couple of days and let you know where we are."

I got out of the car and closed the door. "Listen, be good," said Kittery. "I'll talk to you. Bye."

"Bye," I said, but I don't think she heard me, she accelerated so quickly.

Topsy was still wallpapering when I came in. I found her upstairs in one of the little bedrooms, changing it from green stripes to a patriotic pattern of eagles and drums and bayonets. It smelled of perspiration and paste. She had pushed the iron bed to the middle of the floor, and I lay down on it.

"It's late," she said. "Where have you been?"

"Out," I said. "Around."

"Don't be too specific," Topsy said.

"I was over at Elsa's," I said. "And at Ransom's with John Calvin."

"Actually, I didn't think you'd have the nerve to come home," Topsy said. "After deserting me like that. Thanks a whole lot."

"Sorry," I said. "Kittery just wanted me to go with her."

"Kittery is spoiled rotten. She's too used to getting what she wants."

"I know," I said. I rolled away from Topsy and faced the wall. She had peeled the wallpaper off, but there were still bits hanging on: the green stripes, and beneath that, patches of other, less recent papers. It was like looking down a well. I could hear Topsy smoothing the paper to the wall, squeezing out the pockets of air and lumps of paste. There was a musty bedspread on the bed, and I crawled under it. I remembered about Rocky.

"Guess what?" I asked.

"What?"

"You ran over Rocky."

"Who's Rocky?"

"You know Rocky," I said. "Duane's cat."

"I did no such thing," Topsy said.

"Yes, you did," I said. "Duane told Kittery. You backed over him or something."

"No," said Topsy. "Really?"

"I swear," I said. "At least that's what Duane said."

"Is he dead?"

"Yes."

"Lord," Topsy said. "I knew something terrible was going to happen. I could just feel it."

I could tell she had stopped working by the quiet. I had my head under the bedspread and I lay there for a while, waiting for Topsy to say something. I was thinking of Kittery and Duane driving the mobile home into the night. Maybe they were on the highway by now. In a way I thought they were crazy but in a way I didn't. In a way I wanted to be driving somewhere fast on the highway, but in a way I was glad to be there near my grandmother. For a long time we were both quiet. And then she said, "If you're going to fall asleep, you should get into your own bed."

I didn't answer. I was too tired to respond, let alone get up and go downstairs. Plus, I knew Topsy would wake me up when she finished wallpapering the room, so I could admire it.

THE WINTER BAZAAR

When Bertha Knox died, Knox Farm was developed with "luxury" homes and renamed Norwell Estates. They were the first split-level houses in that part of Indiana, and for a while it was a big deal to visit someone in the Estates to see how the kitchen and living room and bedroom were all on different levels. All that remained of the farm was the house and a couple of acres of cornfields, which belonged to the Methodist Church. Bertha Knox had been a Presbyterian, but the Presbyterians had hired a woman minister, so Mrs. Knox left her house to the Methodists, after her lawyer told her she couldn't leave it to her dog, Mr. Jim.

A man from Gaitlinburg eventually bought the farmhouse and the fields fronting the Range Road from the Methodist Church. His plan was to get the zoning changed and open a Dairy Freeze, but when the selectmen proved uncooperative, he stopped paying his mortgage. The Norwell Valley Savings Bank (the only bank in town) was forced to foreclose on the property. The furnishings of the house had remained in Methodist ownership, and anything that wasn't junk was being sold at the Winter Bazaar.

One morning in early October, Walter Doyle, who was the president of the Norwell Valley Savings Bank, stopped at the farmhouse on his way to the Rotary lunch at McGooley's Tavern, over in Hempel. He only intended to have a quick look around, but something about the abandoned, sunlit rooms entranced him. He went upstairs. The bedrooms were tidy and poised, as if awaiting guests. He couldn't remember when he was last in such a quiet, peaceful place, and the thought of lunch in the basement of McGooley's—the smoke, the sticky floors, the gelatinous beef stew—repulsed him. So he took a bath, a decadently long bath, in the large porcelain bathtub, and then he lay down on one of the beds in his boxer shorts and T-shirt.

When he woke up the sun had passed from the window. For a moment he didn't remember who or where he was. This feeling of disorientation was so rich and transporting he lay still and let it linger. But slowly it faded; his life filtered back into place, familiar and intact. He got dressed and went downstairs.

Mrs. Topsy Hatter, the chairman of the Winter Bazaar Committee, was standing in the kitchen with a carving knife poised in front her. When she saw it was Walter Doyle coming down the stairs, she said, "Jesus, Walter, you scared me."

"Sorry," Walter said.

"How long have you been here?" Topsy put the knife back in a drawer.

She was wrapping glasses in yellowed newspaper. All the cabinet doors were open, arms reaching into the room. The kitchen table was crowded with stemware.

"I fell asleep upstairs," Walter said. "I just stopped by to check things, and I fell asleep. I don't know what's wrong with me."

"You're probably just tired."

Walter didn't know Mrs. Hatter very well, but he had always been a little bit in love with her. He had baby-sat for her kids, Ellen and Knight, twenty-five years ago. Mr. Hatter had died sometime after that. Mrs. Hatter had worked for the phone company, and brought up Ellen's two kids after Ellen fell apart, but they were pretty much grown up now. She still lived in her big old house out on Cobble Road. She was active in the town, but she didn't really fit in with the other ladies. There had always been something competent and independent about her, a way of dismissing things she found irrelevant, that frightened people. Topsy Hatter did things like wear pants and let her black, black hair hang long and loose, back when other women were wearing dresses and getting what they called hairdos at Joanie's every week. Walter was sure Mrs. Hatter had never set a foot inside of Joanie's.

"Are you taking those for the bazaar?" he asked.

"Yes," she said. "You know, Bertha Knox had some nice things. It's kind of sad, her not having anyone to give them to. A stupid dog."

"Can I help?"

"Oh, no," said Topsy. "This is my job. Shouldn't you be at work?"

"They will survive without me." Walter sat down at the kitchen table. He picked up one of the glasses, got up, and filled it at the tap. The water was rusty, but he let it run till it turned clear. It tasted fresher and sweeter than the water at home. It must be well water, he thought.

"You're doing this all yourself?" He sat back down. "Don't you have any helpers?"

"No," said Topsy. "I like it, coming out here. It's nice and quiet. I'll let the ladies take care of the rest, but I like being out here alone."

"It doesn't scare you?"

Topsy laughed. "No," she said. "It doesn't scare me."

"I like being here, too," Walter said.

He watched her swaddle a glass. Her dark hair was gray now, but he couldn't tell how long, since it was in a bun. "You used to have such long hair," he said. "It was beautiful. Is it still?"

"It's still long," she said, "but I don't think it was ever beautiful."

"Can I see it?"

"No," she said.

"Why not?" he asked.

"Because."

He picked up a sheet of the newspaper. It was the *Norwell Bulletin*, ten years old. "Old news," he said.

"I found it in the basement. There are stacks and stacks of them."

"You went down into the basement?" That was where Bertha Knox and Mr. Jim's bodies had been found.

"Apparently."

"You weren't scared?"

"Of what?"

"I don't know. Scared to go down there?"

"No," said Topsy. "I wasn't. I don't scare easy."

The next day he was there when she arrived. She recognized his car behind the hedge and she thought about backing up and leaving, but she didn't. She parked beside it and went inside. He was packing the glasses she had wrapped in a cardboard box.

"What are you doing here?" she asked.

"I'm not here," he said. He smiled. "I'm in Gaitlinburg. I'm meeting with Mr. Angelo Carmichael in Gaitlinburg."

"Who's Mr. Angelo Carmichael?"

"The Dairy Freeze man. We're having lunch."

For a moment Topsy just stood there. She was trying to think things out, think of everything, be logical. But she had trouble concentrating. Walter stood up. He was a handsome man. He opened the refrigerator. From the back he was a large handsome man. The only thing in the fridge was a bottle of wine. He took it out and looked at it as if he were surprised to find it there.

"Would you like a glass of wine?" he asked. He held the bottle out to her, like a waiter in a restaurant, so she could see the label. Only she couldn't see it; she had trouble seeing anything. She sat down.

"Some wine?" Walter asked.

"Don't you think it's a little early for wine?"

Walter looked disappointed. He shrugged. "I guess so," he said. "Maybe later."

"Maybe," Topsy said.

"Do you mind that I'm here?" he asked. He sat down beside her. Topsy didn't answer.

"Do you want me to leave?"

"Maybe I will have a little wine," Topsy said. "Just a touch."

The next day his car was there, and she turned around and drove home, but when she got there she realized she wanted to see him, so she drove back to the farmhouse. But his car was gone.

She didn't think he'd be there the next day, and she was right. She started to sort through the pots and pans. After about half an hour she heard a noise upstairs. It sounded like a bird. She stopped and listened, but she didn't hear anything.

"Walter?" she called.

The noise again: an owl.

She went upstairs and found Walter in the back bedroom, in bed, apparently naked. She stood in the doorway.

"What in God's name are you doing?" she asked.

"Waiting for you?"

"You're a married man, Walter," she said. "What would your wife think of you now?"

"I don't think Virginia is thinking of me now."

"What if she were?"

He looked down at the sheet sloped over his stomach and legs. "She'd think I looked silly," he said.

"She'd be right," Topsy said. She went downstairs.

In a little while he came down. She had spread the pots and pans all across the kitchen floor, and he stopped at the door, looking at the display.

"I'm sorry," he said. "I didn't mean to embarrass you."

"You didn't embarrass me," said Topsy. "You embarrassed yourself."

"You think so?"

"Yes," said Topsy. "I do."

He picked his way through the maze of pots and sat at the table. "I've never been unfaithful," he said.

"Do you want a medal?"

"No," he said. "Just so you know. I mean, I'm not a Don Juan."

Topsy smiled. "I didn't think you were."

"Have you ever been unfaithful?"

"I'm not married," said Topsy.

"I mean when you were."

"It's none of your business," said Topsy.

"That means yes," said Walter. "What about since . . . well, since he died? Have you had . . . affairs?"

"I don't think one has affairs in Norwell."

"You'd be surprised."

"I'm sure I would."

Walter stood up. "Well, I guess I better go."

"I suppose so," said Topsy.

"I guess I shouldn't come back, either."

"It would probably be better."

"O.K.," said Walter. He put his topcoat on, picked up his keys. "Good-bye," he said.

Topsy nodded good-bye.

He got his car out of the garage and drove away. Topsy returned to the pots and pans, scrubbing their heat-stained copper bottoms, but after a while she went upstairs, up into the room. He had made the bed, but badly. Men can't make beds, Topsy thought. She started to remake it, and realized the sheets were still warm from him. She put her hand, palm down, on the bottom sheet. She felt as if she were doing something dangerous. She was standing like that, touching the warm spot, when she heard a car in the driveway. She looked out the window and saw Walter come in the back door. He made owl noises. She stayed still, knowing he would find her.

He did. She stood by the bed, and he stood in the doorway.

"I'm back," he said.

"I see," she said. "I was just . . . making the bed." But she wasn't making the bed. She was standing there, looking at him.

"Are you glad I came back?" he asked.

Topsy waited a moment. She couldn't speak, so she nodded yes.

"Good," he said. He came closer, touched her hair. "Well?" he said.

"Wait," said Topsy. "There have got to be rules."

He took his hand away. "Of course," he said. "Rules. What rules? Tell me."

Topsy tried to think of rules. What would good rules be? "Well," she began. "We can stop whenever we want. Either of us. We can just say 'Stop' and it will be over."

"O.K.," said Walter. "Sure."

"And we both have to remember that you're married. That that comes first. That I don't want you to leave your wife. Is that understood?"

Walter nodded.

"And this is between us. Just us. This is private."

"Of course," said Walter. He sat down on the bed. "Sit down," he said.

"Wait," said Topsy. "I'm still thinking." For a moment neither of them said anything. "I guess that's all," said Topsy. "Can you think of anything else?"

Walter shook his head. "I can't think of anything," he said.

They never made plans. They never called each other. They'd just go, and if the other person showed—well, then. Whoever got there first turned on the electric space heater and waited. If it was Topsy waiting, she continued her bazaar work: cleaning out closets, washing sheets, rummaging in the bookshelves.

They made love and ate sandwiches and drank coffee or wine

and talked. As it got colder, they spent more time in bed and less in the kitchen. They listened to squirrels in the attic. They made love.

Walter often fell asleep, and if he did it was Topsy's responsibility to wake him at three o'clock. One afternoon she was lying in bed between warmth from the space heater and warmth from Walter. She had her eyes closed and was making an effort to stay awake, although she wanted very much to sleep simultaneously with Walter. She could feel him dreaming, his big body pressed against her, his mouth wet at the back of her neck, and she felt that if she slipped into sleep she would find herself in his dream: something about a beach, hot sand, hot sun, water, sky, and birds clamoring in trees. After a while she felt the pressure of his body relax, and she knew he was awake.

"Did you have a good sleep?" she asked.

He answered by pulling her closer. She could feel sweat along her back where his stomach had rested, sweat their bodies had created together. She leaned out of the bed and turned down the space heater. She watched its coils fade from orange to red, heard its *ping ping ping,* and felt a sudden tremor of happiness, of the world stretching out all around her, curved and occurring.

"I'm all hot," she said.

He wasn't talking yet. She tried to turn toward him, but he pressed himself harder against her. He wrapped his arms around her, and moved against her, slowly.

"I'm sweating," she said.

He kissed her back, and licked her spine. His tongue felt cool. She tried again to turn and this time he let her. The blankets slipped away from her and he tried to cover her again but she said, "No. I'm hot."

Even the windows were sweating. Topsy got out of bed and opened one. She turned the heater off. She stood looking out, feeling the cold air on her face. She watched the cornstalks rearrange themselves as something—a dog?—walked through them. Darkness was spilling into the sky from some rip near the horizon.

"Come back to bed," Walter said.

"It's late," she said. "You should go."

"Come back," he said. "I have time."

"Where are you today?" she asked. "What's your excuse for not being at work?"

"You," he said. "Come here. Please."

"Is that what you told Gladys?" Gladys was Walter's secretary.

"Yes," said Walter. "And I told Virginia I wouldn't be home for dinner because I'd be in bed with you."

"What did Virginia say?"

Walter didn't answer. Topsy turned away from the window. He was looking at the ceiling. "What would Virginia think of that?" she asked.

"She wouldn't like it," he said. He looked at her. "Virginia . . . loves me."

"Do you love her?"

"In a way," he said. "In our way, yes."

"What way is that?"

"It's hard to describe," he said.

She came and sat on the bed.

"I'm cold," he said.

She went back over and closed the window. The thing was a dog—she saw it emerge from the corn and run through the trees toward Norwell Estates. Someone was calling it. Dinnertime.

"Did you love . . . what was his name?" Walter asked.

"Who?"

"Your husband."

"Karl," she said. "For a while, yes. And then, no."

"Did you hate him?"

"No," she said.

"That's good," he said. "Sometimes I think Virginia hates me."

"Sometimes she probably does."

"I never hate her. I feel sorry for her, but I don't hate her."

"Why do you feel sorry for her?"

Walter thought for a moment. "Because," he said. "It's a little pathetic. I mean all her good deeds. The Foodmobile and the Morning Doves—"

"What are the Morning Doves?"

"They call up senior citizens every morning to make sure they didn't die overnight. Because of what happened with Bertha Knox." Bertha Knox had been dead for quite a while when the gas man found her in the basement.

"What's pathetic about good deeds?"

"Nothing. I mean, I think it's great how much she does. I'm very proud of her."

"But you said it was pathetic."

"Oh, forget it," said Walter. "I don't want to talk about it."

Topsy came back and sat on the bed. "Sometimes I forget I was married. Isn't that terrible?"

"What do you mean, forget?"

"I just forget. I forget all about Karl. Like it never happened. It's very important when it's happening, but when it's over, it's surprising how little . . . effect it has."

"Did you like being married?"

"Of course. I mean, it was nice, raising a family."

"That would be nice," said Walter.

"Why don't . . . you and Virginia?"

"We've tried," said Walter. "It's very difficult. Both times Virginia got pregnant she miscarried. And I guess we feel a little too old for it now."

"How old are you?"

"Forty-two," said Walter. "Virginia is thirty-eight."

"That's not too old," said Topsy. "I was forty-two when I got Kittery and Dominick."

"But you didn't give birth to them," said Walter.

"No," said Topsy. "Ellen did that." They were quiet a moment, and then Topsy stood up and turned on the light.

"Turn it off," Walter said. "Lie down with me."

"No," said Topsy. "It's time to go home."

"Come lie down. For just a little while. I'm sad."

Topsy turned off the light. In the wake of illumination the room seemed darker than it had before. "Why are you sad?" she asked.

Walter thought for a moment. "I don't know," he said.

Tiny Peterson, the junk man, came with his truck and moved everything Topsy had deemed salable to the Sunnipee Hall. Then he came back and took away what was left: That was the junk. There had been a lot of it, and Topsy knew there was no reason to save it for the rummage sale in May. She had learned from experience that there are some things no one will buy, things in this world—often fine things—that are superfluous. That make the mistake of becoming unowned.

A few nights later she and Walter had dinner together in the emptied farmhouse. Virginia was visiting her niece in Dayton. In the darkness of the kitchen everything was black and white except for the red sheen of wine in the glasses on the table.

"This was a bad idea," Topsy said. "I've been meaning to tell you something."

"What?"

"Well, I feel funny about coming here now," Topsy said. She picked up a wineglass and looked at it. "Now that there's no work to do."

"There's still work to do," Walter said. "Our private work."

"No," said Topsy. "I don't feel right about it anymore."

"You mean, it's all right to have an affair if it's accompanied by church-work and not O.K. if it's not?"

"No," said Topsy. "I just mean being here."

"But this is the perfect place. You know it is."

"Well, we can't come here forever. Eventually someone will buy it, won't they?"

"Not if I can help it," said Walter.

"Well, I didn't really mean the place, anyway," Topsy said.

"What did you mean?" Walter stood up. He took the glass of wine from her and drank from it.

"I meant . . . us. I think we should think about ending it."

"Why?"

"What do you think? What do you think about ending it?"

"I don't want to end it," said Walter. He leaned against the sink. "Do you?"

"I think it might be a good idea."

"Why?"

"Well, because. Because I'm starting to depend on it. I'm starting to depend on you."

"What's wrong with that?"

"I don't like it. It's not what I wanted. I didn't want to get attached."

"Are you?"

Topsy looked across the kitchen at him. He was just a dark figure in the shadows, but she could picture him. "I think I am," she said.

"So am I," he said.

"Then we should end it," she said. "Remember the rule?"

"What rule?"

"That you're married. That we wouldn't . . . get fond of each other."

"But we were always fond of each other. Right from the start. At least I was of you." He drank the rest of the wine and put the glass in the sink, then came over and sat next to her. "Why can't we just keep going and see what happens?"

"No," she said. "It will only get worse."

"So let it get worse."

"I don't want it to get worse," Topsy said. "I want to end it now."

He stood up. "I thought you weren't scared. You told me you weren't easily scared."

Topsy shrugged. "I guess I was wrong," she said.

Two weeks later, Topsy stood behind the cashier's table at the Winter Bazaar and watched Walter Doyle walk up and down the aisles. He arrived at the cashier's with a tackle box full of lures and weights.

"Those are twenty-five cents apiece," Topsy said.

"Do I get a discount if I buy them all?"

"I guess so," said Topsy.

"How about five dollars?"

"You want the box, too?"

"Of course," said Walter.

"Five dollars for the contents, and five dollars for the box. Ten for it all."

"This box isn't worth five dollars," said Walter. "Not even brand-new."

"Eight dollars, then," Topsy said. "For everything."

"O.K.," said Walter. He gave her a ten-dollar bill.

"Do you want your change? Any amount over your purchase price is a tax-deductible contribution."

"I'll take my change," said Walter.

Topsy gave him two tired dollar bills.

"You've got quite a crowd," he said. "How's it going?"

"We need buyers."

"Virginia's coming this afternoon. She's a buyer. Is that coffee free?"

"A nickel."

"What about a free cup for purchases eight dollars and over?"

"It's a nickel, Walter."

Walter extracted a dime from his pants pocket. "Keep the

change," he said. "That's tax-deductible, right?"

Topsy poured him a cup of coffee.

"Are cream and sugar extra?" he asked.

"Help yourself," said Topsy.

Walter drank his coffee and watched Topsy fill a tray of paper cups with juice. She arranged all the cups with their edges touching, and then poured the juice down the rows in one long swoop, filling each cup perfectly, spilling none.

"Looks like you've done that before," Walter said.

"Just one of my many talents," said Topsy.

"Do you have a lost-and-found?" asked Walter.

"What did you lose?"

"A . . . glove."

"There's a box in the kitchen," Topsy said. "But I haven't seen any men's gloves."

"Could we look?"

"It's in the kitchen. Go ahead."

"Come with me."

"I have to stay here."

"You could get someone to cover for you, couldn't you?"

"I don't see the point. I'm sure you can find your own glove. If you did, indeed, lose it."

"'Indeed'?"

"What?"

"Since when do you say, 'did, indeed'?" Topsy shrugged. She drank a glass of juice. "Since now," she said.

"As a matter fact, I didn't, indeed, lose a glove."

"I thought not."

"You thought not?"

"Stop it, Walter."

"Well, why are you talking like that?"

"Like what?"

"Like . . . you don't like me."

"I'm not. I don't."

"Don't what?"

"Don't not like you."

"I don't not like you either."

A child interrupted them to buy a deflated beach ball and a transistor radio shaped like a frog.

"I miss you," said Walter, when the transaction had been completed. "Do you miss me?"

"I try not to," said Topsy.

"But you do?"

"A little."

"How much?"

"I told you: a little."

"Don't lie."

"I'm not lying. I don't lie."

Walter felt like saying, yeah, you don't get scared, either, but he didn't. Instead he said, "Are you sure?"

"Walter, stop it. Please. I'm not going to discuss this in the church hall."

"Will you discuss it somewhere else?"

"No. It's pointless."

Walter threw his empty coffee cup into the garbage can. He picked up his tackle box. "Here," he said. "I don't really want this." He put the box down on the table.

"Take it," said Topsy. "You paid for it."

"I don't want it. I don't fish."

"Well, then, let me give you your money back." She took eight dollars out of the box and held them out, but Walter was walking toward the door. She looked at the money in her hand, then put it back in the cash box.

When Virginia Doyle came in later that afternoon, Topsy deducted eight dollars from her grand total. When Virginia asked why, Topsy said they were just giving discounts to good customers. Virginia looked at her as if she were crazy. She told her that was no way to run a church bazaar.

*   *   *

For a while after Topsy stopped seeing Walter, she avoided driving past Knox Farm. If she were going over to Hempel she took the long way, out to the end of Cobble Road and back around through Gaitlinburg. But one day—the first day it was warm enough to drive with the windows open—she found that she had forgotten to take the long way; that she was on the Range Road, and the next thing she knew she was driving up the dirt road to the farmhouse. For a few minutes she just sat in the car, not knowing what she wanted to do. She had tried to park out of sight and when she opened the windows wider an overgrown arm of forsythia unfurled into the car. The thin stalk was speckled with wartlike, pale green buds; it bobbed in front of her face. She opened her mouth and set her lips to it. She bit a little so she could taste its bitterness. She closed her eyes. She thought about her life and how things happened in it, how you couldn't stop things from happening or control them. It was as if you and all the things that could possibly happen in your life were floating in a pool the size of an ocean and you only touched some of them, and it was all accidental, and the things you wanted were as slim and slippery as fish. Fish swam between your fingers and legs and brushed against your sides; silver-sided fish nibbled at your toes; shy, skittish fish flitted to the surface and then flipped away, no matter how still you stood, no matter how quiet you were, for they could sense your desire: It pulsed from you like sonar—*come to me, come to me, come to me*—driving the swarms of swimming things far away.

In early summer, when the days were like balm, Topsy drove to the Norwell Valley Savings Bank and climbed the stairs to Walter's office. Gladys Wallace was feeding a pencil to an electric sharpener.

"Hello, Gladys," Topsy said.

"Well, hi, Mrs. Hatter. What can we do for you?"

"Is Walter in?"

"Mr. Doyle? He's in a meeting at the moment. Did you have an appointment?"

No, I don't. But maybe you could tell Walter—Mr. Doyle—that I'm here. He told me to stop by anytime."

"O.K., I'll let him know. Will you excuse me?"

"I sure will," said Topsy. She sat in an easy chair and picked up a copy of *Colonial Homes.*

Gladys reappeared shortly, closing the door behind her as if she had just got a baby down inside. "He says he'll see you now," she said. "You can go right in."

"Thanks," said Topsy. She went in Walter's office and closed the door, a little less quietly than Gladys had. "Hello, Walter," she said.

Walter nodded. He looked a little stunned.

"They climb out the window?" Topsy asked.

"Who?" asked Walter.

"The folks you were meeting with. Gladys told me you were in a meeting."

"I wasn't," said Walter.

"I guessed not," said Topsy.

"I'm in a meeting sometimes," said Walter.

"I'm sure you are," said Topsy. She sat down. For a moment neither of them said anything. They heard Gladys resume her pencil-sharpening. "Don't you want to know why I'm here?" Topsy asked.

"I was wondering," said Walter. "Although it's nice to see you."

Topsy snorted. "I'm here on business," she said. "I want to buy Knox Farm. I'm going to sell my house."

"Why?" asked Walter.

"Why what?"

"Why are you going to sell your house?"

"It's too big."

"Knox Farm isn't small."

Topsy smiled. "This is business, Walter," she said. "I just want to buy a house your bank happens to own."

"Well, how much are you offering?"

"I'd like to see it," said Topsy.

"I thought you had."

"I'd like to see it again. Before I make an offer."

"Oh," said Walter. "I guess that seems fair."

"Maybe you'd drive out there with me? Show it to me?"

They looked at each other for a moment. Then Walter stood up and put on his jacket. "Certainly," he said. "I don't see why not."

Walter opened the back door with a key that was hidden in the milk box. They went into the kitchen. The only thing in it was sunlight.

"This is the kitchen," Walter said. He turned on the faucet; rusty water flowed into the sink. "Running water," he announced.

"Stop it," said Topsy.

Walter turned off the water and shrugged. "What do you want?" he asked. "What are we doing here?"

"I just wanted to talk to you," Topsy said.

"Oh," said Walter.

"I'm lonely," said Topsy.

Walter didn't respond. He didn't want to look at her so he opened a silverware drawer, looked in at its emptiness.

"I can't stand . . . being lonely like this," he heard her say. "I mean, I was lonely before you, but I never realized. It wasn't till we were together—well, after, when we stopped—that I realized . . ."

Inside the drawer an ant walked across a field of green felt. It climbed over a cork and paused at the summit. Walter decided to pretend he hadn't heard what Topsy had said. Once decided, it was easy.

After a moment, he said, "Did you really want to buy the house?"

"No," said Topsy. "Well, maybe for a minute. It was just an idea. A dumb idea."

"It's not a bad house," Walter said. He closed the drawer and wiped his hands together. He stood up straighter. "Well, then," he said. "I guess we should be going." He jiggled his car keys.

Topsy didn't move. "You go," she said. "It's O.K. I want to stay for a while."

"How will you get home?"

"I'll walk. Go."

He looked around the kitchen as if instructions for how to act might be displayed somewhere, like a choking poster. "I'm sorry," he said. "It's not that I don't want to stay . . ."

"I didn't expect you to stay. I don't know what I thought. Please, go."

"No. I mean, I still feel the—I still feel for you. I do. It's just that, well, things are better with Virginia. We've worked some things out. I mean, we're trying. And I don't think I should—"

"It's all right." She looked up at him and smiled. "That's good for you. I'm happy."

Walter studied his keys as if they were unfamiliar to him. "Are you sure you don't want a ride?"

"It's a nice day to walk," she said.

"O.K., then," he said. He moved toward her, as if he might embrace her, but then walked around her, out the door. She waited till his car had pulled away, till the sound of it was gone, before she moved. She went upstairs and walked through the rooms, looked out the bedroom window. The same cornstalks were still standing patiently in the field. She didn't feel particularly sad. She felt numb.

Eventually she went back downstairs. Walter had left the key in the door. She thought about taking it as a souvenir, but then she realized she didn't want one. She locked the door and tossed the key into the milk box, kicked the lid shut with her foot, and started walking home.